Great Escapes
from Detroit

Praise for
Joseph O'Malley

"Joseph O'Malley writes about ordinary people with such care and a clear eye for the truth. The stories in *Great Escapes from Detroit* are luminous with what lesser writers miss—the magic and the splendor of the commonplace come alive."

–Lee Martin, author of The Bright Forever

Great Escapes

from Detroit

stories by
Joseph O'Malley

Cornerstone Press
Stevens Point, Wisconsin

Cornerstone Press, Stevens Point, Wisconsin 54481
Copyright © 2019 Joseph O'Malley
www.uwsp.edu/cornerstone

Printed in the United States of America by:
Worzalla Publishing, Stevens Point, Wisconsin 54481

Library of Congress Control Number: 2019951287
ISBN: 978-1-7333086-1-8

Cornerstone Press titles are produced in courses and internships offered by the
Department of English at the University of Wisconsin–Stevens Point.

DIRECTOR & PUBLISHER   EXECUTIVE EDITOR   DEVELOPMENT COORDINATOR
Dr. Ross K. Tangedal   Jeff Snowbarger   Alexis Neeley

SENIOR PRESS ASSISTANTS
Monica Swinick, Katy Nachampassak, Madeline Swanger

FALL 2019 STAFF
McKenna Rentmeester, Olivia Frome, Jeremy Wolfe, Heidi Propson, Tori Schuler,
Aleesha Splinter, Brendan Gallert, Johanna Honore, Emma King, Dartaja Carr, Dillon
Lehrer, Ali Zamzow, Logan Christie, Moira Eisenman, Reggie Kelnhoffer, Sarah Lundy,
Jerry Markarian, Shane McNealy, Dylan Morey, Kyle Pluemer, Cody Striegel, Brianna
Stumpner, Super Vang

For my family

Contents

TOO BEAUTIFUL

When her father arrived home from his wanderings down between the expressway and the river, and after she had thanked the Misses Johnson and Jackson—the retired correctional officers who lived next door—for finding him, Martha decided to take advantage of the high mid-day sun by trimming the lawn, and finally planting those marigolds in the front bushes. Her head was buzzy with nerves and the handfuls of chocolates she'd eaten waiting for "the girls" to find her father again and bring him home in one piece. As usual the police were no help, and how he always got so far with the limp and that ulcer on his leg Martha never knew.

It was her day off from the Doll Hospital where she routinely dismembered and reassembled the limbs of the dear little loved ones of dear little loved ones. She knew she wasn't kidding anyone; it was Martha's idea to scrawl "Doll Hospital" on a neatly trimmed piece of cardboard to hang over the proper "Repair Dept." sign at her job in the doll factory. The factory sat next to one of several abandoned auto parts plants in a windowless brick building perched on the murky waters that sludged past a downriver suburb of Detroit. It had been a year since her demotion from Production to Repair after they'd successfully traced the string of cross-eyed Perky Suzie dolls to her station for the second time, and told her they would place several unmarked "sniffer" employees to closely watch her work in Repair. Whatever powers Martha could summon to spruce up the less inspiring aspects of her life, she used, so when she spoke of her move at work as a boon, and referred to herself as the Surgeon General at the Doll Hospital, Miss Jackson and Miss Johnson were kind enough never to second guess her. In fact, Miss Jackson and Miss Johnson were very, very kind to her; they watched Martha's father on the days she worked, and they refused any pay.

"He keeps us company, is all," Miss Jackson said in her Kentucky drawl, and Miss Johnson said, "Yeah," which is about as much as she ever said.

Martha was beginning to take personally the fact that her father only wandered away when she was home; she worried it made her look like a sloppy daughter--careless for sleeping in until eight o'clock just because it was her day off.

When they finally brought him home, Miss Johnson calmed Martha's tears with a firm hand on her shoulder. Miss Jackson bent to look Martha's father in the eye. "Stay put now. Okay, Joe?" She leaned in further and placed her pig-pink cheek against his stubbled face for a long moment, then stood up straight and let Miss Johnson lead her home by the arm.

"Good Christ, Dad," Martha said. "You must be exhausted." She kissed him on the forehead and led him toward the couch. "Do you want a nap?"

He looked at her with one eye milky from the cataract and one eye bright and slick from his overabundantly lubricated sockets. He hesitated and stared hard at her, his eyes searching for something. Finally he said, "Martha?"

"Yes!" she said. "That's right, Dad, I'm Martha," and when she laughed, he did too. She sat him down on the couch and let him lie back. She let go of his hand. Another wave of contractions flitted over his face and he said, "Julia?"

"No Dad," Martha said. She picked up his hand to kiss, then relinquished it to let it rest over his chest. "That's Mom. She's been gone for years. I'm Martha. Get some rest."

He reached his hand up again and held it against her face. Soon enough his focus receded, his arm wilted back into place over his own chest, and he nodded off.

Although she was sure he'd never be able to climb the back fence, she locked and bolted the back door just in case. His capabilities and reserves of energy surprised her more and more, as the morning had proven. Two miles away!

She locked the front door until she'd gotten the seeds, the flats of marigolds, the weedwacker with the extension cord, and the small gardening rake and trowel out of the garage. Then she opened the front door to let some air in through the screen, and in case he woke and wanted to sit in one of the lawn chairs on the front porch to keep her company later.

Even with her head between the bushes Martha could hear her other next-door neighbor rumbling awake. Her name was Kim. "Kimmy, for short," she'd told Martha the day Kim and her husband moved in three years earlier; they were new to the neighborhood where Martha had lived her whole life, and because Kim was young and pretty and pregnant, Martha didn't have the heart to correct her. Now she knew better. Kimmy got away with far too much because of that pouty angel face of hers.

Kim's three small kids had been out tearing up and down the sidewalk on Big Wheels for hours. Martha heard something being hurled or kicked through the house next door. She tried to ignore it while she loosened the dull smelling earth. She dug down into its soft coolness with her bare hands, and crumbled wads of dirt while feeling for stones and the roots of weeds. She plopped the stones into a coffee can, and shook the weeds free of dirt before stuffing them into a small plastic K-Mart bag to discard later.

After a while she straightened her back, sat on her heels, and peered over at Kimmy's front yard. Large yellow-brown spots dotted the lawn. Kimmy's habit of weakly tossing bags of garbage from her front porch to let them lay where they landed for five or six days until garbage night had leeched any sign of life from the crab grass and dandelions that otherwise grew in copious profusion there. When garbage night finally did arrive, she ordered her son, seven-year-old Dylan, and his younger sister, five-year-old Heather, to drag the bags to the curb. The baby, apparently, was still too young for manual labor.

Sometimes the bags would break, and on windy days the refuse would swirl about and land on Martha's lawn.

The one time Martha complained to Kimmy about her unorthodox habits, Kimmy twitched her mouth into an electric thin line, widened her eyes, and said, "I've got three kids to worry about. I don't have a daddy to take care of me, and I don't have time to worry about garbage."

Kimmy's way of saying exactly what she thought without first passing it through an adult filter of civility rankled Martha. She had never experienced anything like it. Martha had heard there was medication to remedy that kind of thing, but she thought suggesting to a neighbor that she seek professional help might be pushing the envelope a tad too far. What Martha couldn't get used to, she tried to ignore; sometimes this method worked and sometimes it didn't. The garbage issue became a sticking point for them.

In her more generous moments, Martha saw that Kim deserved a little sympathy. She was a person just like Martha with struggles of her own, and when Kim and her husband had first moved in Martha had even found her charming. She'd had to admit Kim was a very pretty woman, with her long, straight blond hair, and her body, which was shapely and looked slightly underweight but healthy, even when pregnant. On first impression Dylan and Heather were adorable, and Martha knew that for some reason it was wrong to dislike a pregnant woman. The husband had seemed a bit of a goof even then, but Martha shrugged off her criticisms with a sigh and a silent oh well.

Then the hijinks started: the loud parties in the backyard, the drinking, and the smoking of skunky smelling marijuana until all hours. The habit Kim had of speaking about "the blacks" in the neighborhood with a nod and a nudge in her voice made Martha blink in discomfort, and there were also the snide remarks about Miss Jackson and Miss Johnson, which especially pained Martha now. She'd laughed heartily at Kimmy's slights, and even offered not only an imitation of Miss Jackson's hunched galumphing walk, but also of the crude way Miss Johnson had of holding a finger to one nostril and blowing a wad of snot out the other onto the sidewalk. Kim's children walked around with bags under their eyes from lack of sleep, and became cranky and aggressive. They threw sticks and stones--literally! sticks! stones!-- over the backyard fence and called Martha "Biggie Biggie Lady." Then came the scarecrow-looking people who mistook Martha's house for Kim's and pounded on the front door at three, four, five o'clock in the morning shouting in unintelligible grunts. All this happened a while after Martha noticed her forgetful father forgetting more important things: recent conversations, the names of old friends and relatives, how to tie his own shoelaces.

Two and a half years had passed this way, and now the husband was in jail. With her head bent low to give the impression of shame, Kimmy had told Martha, "for drugs. Hard drugs." Now that the husband was gone, Martha finally understood that he had not been solely to blame for the chaos next door, as Kimmy had hinted. The husband had been incarcerated at the beginning of March, and the garbage issue started as soon as spring broke. The first time it happened, the kids stood on the porch crying because Kim had locked them out. Finally Kim opened the door and flung Dylan's Big Wheel out the door over his head. "Garbage!" she screamed. Dylan's eyes, the same singed reddish brown color as his hair, watched the Big Wheel fly, but his head never moved. Next came a doll house. Heather, a towheaded blond like her mother, with hair that curled around her pretty face like tumbleweed, watched Barbie's Ski Chateau crack and split apart on the pavement. "Garbage!" Kim shouted, and her voice grew more frantic with the trajectory of each object. Although alarmed, Martha did not call the police because there was no real crime to report.

Later came the quiet, which lasted all afternoon and into the evening, and Martha relaxed a little. Around midnight, Kim's banshee wail hooked through the night air to jerk Martha awake. Her first impulse was to check on her father to be sure he hadn't wandered into somebody's bedroom or bathroom to catch an unsuspecting neighbor in the middle of a compromising situation. She found her father sound asleep. Martha returned to her own bedroom on the second floor and looked out the window. Across the way she could see into Kim's house. In Kim's bedroom, also on the second floor, all the lights flared up bright as searchlights, and the radio blasted. Kimmy stormed back and forth across the room in a bra and panties, throwing things. The kids continued to cry, Kimmy stomped down the stairs, the crashing noises acquired a rhythm. Martha decided to call the police when she heard Dylan's voice bellowing in what sounded like a response to certain torture. The louder he screamed the louder and more frequent came the crashing noises.

When Kimmy returned to the bedroom, Martha crouched low beneath her sill and watched, hidden, she thought, by the darkness of her own room and the blindness that she felt sure was inherent in Kimmy's rage. But at one point Kimmy spun around to look straight in Martha's direction. She picked up the radio and flung it through her window directly at Martha's head. The radio flew through the small space between the houses, its cord trailing like the tail of a wild animal. Luckily, the radio bounced off Martha's screen to resolve itself with a clatter into a junk heap of sprung springs and cracked plastic on the cement patio tiles outside Kim's back door. "Garbage!" Kimmy screamed, and Martha no longer had any doubt that Kimmy's ire was directly aimed at her.

Martha crawled to the stairs and descended, called 911 again, and peeked through the front curtains to wait for the police. She had the foresight to open the window in her bathroom just a crack, since that window was directly across from Kim's back door, where it turns out, the police knocked. Martha watched at a safe angle, sitting comfortably on the carpet of her living room floor peering out from under the blind. She could hear everything as the policemen's voices wafted in through the bathroom window.

Kimmy greeted the police in her bra and panties. With her long blond hair and a body more like that of a teenager than of a mother of three, she gave the police her sob story of being a single mother trying to scrape by on unemployment, with bratty kids and nosey neighbors.

She laughed, and swayed her tight skin against the night breeze for the two tall men in blue.

And guess what? The police were no help. "Well," they told her, "try to keep it down."

After the police left, Kimmy set up camp by the upstairs window, strutting and posing in front of it as though it were a mirror. Martha crouched trembling beneath the sill, yet couldn't help but watch.

"People!" Kimmy yelled staring into the dark between their houses. "People hate me because I'm beautiful. People don't know how hard it is to be beautiful." She shook her head so her hair flew every which way, blurring like the blades in a fan as she gathered momentum with each phrase she uttered. "I'm beautiful on the inside!" She stomped her foot. "And I'm beautiful on the outside!" Her hands splayed out from her sides and moved as frantically as her hair. "I'm too beautiful for words. People don't know how hard it is..." She stopped thrashing about and appeared to make an effort to stand still, but her whole body shook in spasms as if she were being electrocuted. "To beee... Sooooo... Beautifuuuuuuuuuul!!!" She howled into the night like a cat in heat.

Two days later she was contrite and charming again, but Martha never knew how long her sedate moods would last. Kimmy hung her head in that way she had of pouting her lower lip and looking up between her bangs. The paradox of a truly disarming charm was Kim's most shocking trait, and not only because it contrasted so greatly with her savage moods, which had escalated in both frequency and intensity over the past year. Martha never doubted the sincerity of Kim's gentle rationality when in its presence; it was only after they returned to their respective homes and Martha had a chance to think more about it, to parse out what might be real and what faked, that doubt entered.

The week after the flying radio incident, Kim knocked on Martha's door holding her little girl's hand and carrying in her other hand a box of homemade orange blossom meringues, Kim's own recipe. "Sorry about the other night," Kim said. She handed over the meringues to Martha. "I think you like these," she said, and Martha recalled with a pang the day she'd visited Kim just after the husband had gone into the clink. The full plate of meringues had sat between them, and when Martha left half an hour later she noticed she'd eaten every last meringue off the plate without realizing it. She'd hoped Kim hadn't noticed.

Martha did not want to be taken in again by Kim's charm, or her own sweet tooth.

"About the other night," Kim said. She paused, let go of her daughter's hand to stroke her own forehead. "Migraines," Kim said. "I get migraines and.... Well, I can't describe it."

"Oh," was all Martha wanted to say, but some stupid quality in her that always wanted things smoothed over made her say, "That's okay," even though it wasn't.

After Kim had left, Martha ate all the meringues in one sitting. Only after the sugar kicked in and she could count the throb of her pulse by touching her tongue against the gums at the back of her teeth did she realize she'd missed her opportunity to broach the topic of lawn care—a gentle suggestion to clean it up. Just because they lived in Detroit and were poor didn't mean they had to look and act poor. She knew she should have had the conversation the day Kim apologized, but she'd missed her chance, and in the month since then Kim had kept herself cooped up in the house. Martha saw her only once that month, when Kim and the kids carried groceries from the car to the house, their heads bent low to keep from having to say hello.

She had half a mind to clean up Kim's yard herself by stealth in the middle of the night, but Miss Jackson and Miss Johnson cautioned against this.

"She don't care," Miss Jackson said. They stood talking on Martha's porch one day after Martha returned home from work.

"Nope," said Miss Johnson. "Not a nit. Don't care."

"She'd just expect it anyways if you did it for her."

"Surely she will. Just make it worse."

Martha's father, hand transferred firmly from Miss Jackson's hand to Martha's, looked around and over his shoulder at something, or for something, it was always hard to tell. The three women looked over at the tangled mess of Kimmy's yard.

"Damn shame though," said Miss Jackson.

"Mmnn!" said Miss Johnson.

"Shameful," Miss Jackson said again.

They shook their heads, jangled the keys on the chains that attached to large black leather wallets in their back pockets, and returned home.

Martha truly respected neighbors who recognized the importance of lawn care. Miss Jackson and Miss Johnson kept their lawn like they kept their hair: trimmed to within an inch of its life. It was they who had taught Martha the pleasures of the weedwacker to keep the borders of the lawn militarily precise, but they didn't go in for flowers. Instead they opted for berry bushes that skirted the perimeter of their house, which was painted completely white. White shutters, white rain gutters, white siding, white porch. They'd even painted the cement walk that led up to their porch white.

On each side of Martha's porch three evergreen bushes shot up almost as high as the windows. She trimmed them thin to showcase an array of tall and short flowers between the marigolds, which kept away the mosquitoes.

An orderly row of marigolds under the evergreens would have been attractive enough on its own, but the rest of the flowers brought vivacity to an otherwise drab neighborhood; she surprised and delighted herself and her neighbors with the wild combinations of flowers that popped up as the season wore on into summer. She knew she set herself up for ridicule by taking pictures of her full-blown garden and bringing them in to work to show to her coworkers the way other people brought in pictures of their stupid children. Every year she fought the impulse, and every year she lost the fight, took two rolls of pictures, and when she heard people laughing, then saw the way they abruptly stopped and looked at her with their breaths held when she walked into the room, and saw the pitiful expressions on their faces--pitying her!--she renewed her vow, tore up the pictures, and scattered them out the window over the highway on the drive home from work.

Still, one had to have pride.

Martha rehearsed many subtle hints she could give Kim in regard to yard care. If she really thought she was beautiful on the inside and beautiful on the outside, she could show it in the way she kept her house. "Show some pride," Martha thought she might say to Kim, but since that implied the opposite, she kept her own counsel. In the end, she thought it best to lead by example.

So she got down on her knees and began.

After an hour of weeding, her sun bonnet drooped, wilted by the considerable sweat collecting at the rim, and her arms and legs blotched red despite the sunscreen. She tried to wipe away the sweat that had gathered in her eyebrows with the back of her arm so she wouldn't smear dirt all over her face with her hands--she never completely succeeded in this. She'd successfully blocked out the rumbling noises from next door, but could not quite escape the agitation that looking at Kimmy's yard caused.

Once, on a television nature special, Martha had seen a hawk pouncing on a desert rat, and the sudden scream that rang from Kimmy's house sounded just like that. It scared Martha half to death. She lifted her sun-bonneted head slightly from the bushes to listen.

"I told you NOT to eat that in here. Now you've dropped it on the carpet. Peanut butter on the CARPET! Look at it. LOOK. AT. IT. If you think I'm going to clean that up, you're crazy."

Kimmy burst through her front door onto the porch wearing a pastel pink and green bikini. She pranced off the porch and got down on her hands and knees in front of the patch of dirt next to it filled with coarse bracken and thistle that never flowered. She began to yank and to yank and to yank, with a little scream accompanying each yank. The sun bore down directly on her, having no tree or bush to filter it.

Martha felt she had taken enough chances watching Kim. She burrowed more deeply into the bushes contemplating the mixed blessing her example seemed to have wrought. At least the girl was making an effort. Martha's knees sank into the dirt she'd just cultivated. She grabbed for the spindly clover and a weed with big jagged leaves that she wasn't sure wasn't poisonous, but oh well, you take your chances in this life.

Kimmy's yelps submerged into a long, low growl punctuated by an occasional shouted word, and it was the occasional word Martha hoped to catch. Martha slowed her progress through the weeds and stared at the soil beneath her in an attempt to concentrate on what Kimmy was saying.

"Mind," Martha thought she heard, or maybe it was "Mine." The flats of marigolds were lined up in a row on the lawn behind Martha. She reached back to get a flat and caught a glimpse of Kimmy. The girl didn't even have the sense to shake the weeds free from dirt before flinging them behind her. Great clods of dirt rose, flew, and dropped. Martha distinctly heard the word "Fat," and a short while later, "Father," and her back stiffened. She could straighten, stand and confront Kimmy, or she could let it slide "like water off a duck's back" as her father used to say. She decided to let it slide.

Because Kimmy was throwing the dirt behind her, the silty residue settled, mingled with her sweat, and ran in muddy streams down her shoulders and back making her look more and more wild.

"Minding my own business," Kimmy muttered. "Yard." In a singsong lisp she said, "Beautiful flowers."

Martha finished the weeding and prepared the soil on both sides of the porch for the potted flowers and the seeds. "Police," she heard Kimmy say. Martha moved to the northern side of the porch, the side nearest Kimmy's house, to dig the holes she needed to transplant the marigolds. "Trying," shouted Kimmy into the dirt. Out of the corner of her eye Martha saw her sit up. Kimmy spoke to the front of the house as if it were an altar and she was giving witness. "Some people have everything done for them. I have to do everything myself!" She growled, actually growled.

Martha finished her hole digging quickly and moved to the other side of the porch; she figured it would be better to let Kimmy's fury wear itself out without her to fuel it. Then Kimmy's screen door slammed and all was quiet for a second or two. From inside the house Martha heard Kimmy's shouts. "Flowers. Huh! Pretty! That's all." These short, disconnected phrases mingled with indistinguishable mumbles that gurgled from her throat until she finally said, "Big fat face!"

Martha plopped one plant in each hole and strategically scattered the seeds to assure an interesting yield. She had mixed the seeds, but segregated those flowers that grew very tall, which she planted at the back, from those flowers that were typically short, which she planted closer to the front, near the marigolds. She covered all her seeds with dirt and mulch, then went in to make some lunch, check on her father, and rest a little before she edged the lawn.

The sun, though shrinking, threw off heat more intensely as it slid into its three o'clock slot in the afternoon sky. Whatever green had been left in the ragged excuse for vegetation Kimmy had pulled and tossed onto her lawn had finally seeped out; the husks of weeds were beginning to wilt and curl. All was quiet.

Martha fitted the extension cord onto the weed-wacker's plug, threaded the cord through a slot in one of the kitchen's small windows, and plugged it into the outlet there. The machine itself was ingenious; she couldn't thank Miss Jackson and Miss Johnson enough for introducing her to it. She held it by the long handle and aimed the circular wacker with its metal guard at the edge of the lawn she wanted to trim and, viola!, a rather long strip of plastic or nylon with a knot tied at the end flew out like a cutting tongue and slashed the jagged ends off the edges of the lawn; the end result not only looked better than if she had done it with a spade, but it took about a quarter of the time.

Martha took advantage of the quiet on the northern front. She unfurled the extension cord. A foot path--a strip of concrete about eighteen inches wide that led to Kimmy's back gate--separated Kimmy's lawn from Martha's. Martha wanted to dispatch her side quickly. She revved up the wacker simply by pressing an orange button on the handle. She'd finished the part right near Kimmy's back door quickly, moved smoothly to the part where her own bushes began, and with a sigh of relief was looking forward to the long stretch that led to the front sidewalk when Kimmy slammed the back door and twisted the knob connected to the garden hose. The sprinkler in her front yard, which Martha had not noticed amid the other junk collected there, sprang to life squirting streams of water high into the air and onto Martha and her lawn.

Martha turned off the wacker, and Kimmy turned to stare at Martha with her hands on her hips.

"Kim," Martha said.

Kimmy mimicked her by twisting her face and mouth. "Martha." She folded her arms and canted one hip. There was not even the pretense of common civility.

"I'm only going to be a minute," Martha said, trying to remain calm. It felt like talking to a child. "Could you turn the sprinkler off for just a few minutes?"

"MY lawn needs water," Kimmy said.

"Well, could you maybe not use the sprinkler just yet? I need to get this done."

"I'm not stopping you."

"It's dangerous." Martha lifted the extension cord and flipped it away from the water. "This is electricity, you know?"

Kimmy toggled her head like one of those nodding toys one sees in the backs of people's car windows. She was a full-grown child. Martha could see that now. What had happened or not happened to Kimmy in her youth to make her such a basket case of an adult?

"Oh, all right,' Kimmy finally said. She turned off the water, marched out front to unscrew the sprinkler from the hose, and marched back to turn the hose back on.

"Better?" she sneered.

Martha bit her tongue and revved up the wacker.

Dylan stepped out onto the porch with a toy car in his hand. Behind him followed Heather holding a pink parasol with yellow flowers stuck on it. Kimmy pointed at them and shrilled, "Stay there! I'm doin' the lawn. I don't want you down here." Even over the wacker noise, Martha heard Kimmy clearly. The kids made themselves comfortable on the porch and watched their mother and Martha only a few feet apart intently ignoring one another. Kimmy's back was to Martha. She couldn't tell if the bones and muscles of Kim's back were tense or just tight because she was young and thin, but Martha decided she'd take her time, and if the noise of the weed-wacker bothered Kim, Martha's only regret was that it wasn't louder.

Kimmy lazily waved the hose back and forth over her own lawn while Martha edged her way toward the front sidewalk. Kimmy made some excuse to yell at the kids, and when she did, she jerked the hose so that it soaked Martha's bare leg and sneaker.

"Kim!" Martha said.

Kimmy looked surprised, then disgusted. She straightened her posture to accentuate her breasts. "What's the big deal? It's just a little water. It won't kill you."

Martha released the rev button on the wacker, and briefly inspected her wet shoe. Looking pale and feeling lumpen and mean, she noticed the pucker her dirty knees made in the flesh of her legs. She heard her own screen door slam, and turned to see her father standing on the porch.

"Dad," she said. She snapped her fingers, pointed to one of the lawn chairs on the porch. He dutifully sat.

"Daddy, Daddy," Kim mocked.

Martha ignored her taunts and got to the point. "Look, Kim. If you could just wait for ten minutes, I'll be finished and you can water all you like." She heard her own voice losing all authority as it rose in pitch.

"Why should I have to wait for you?" Kimmy said. "I've got a million things to do. I've got three kids to take care of. All by myself. I don't live with my daddy."

Martha looked at her father and pointed to him. "I've got plenty to do, too."

"What?" said Kimmy. "He's just crazy. Poor you, with your crazy papa."

Martha's father stood up and held onto the aluminum porch railing under the awning. "Don't talk to her," he said. With more emphasis, he added, "Her."

"Dad!" Martha said. She was losing patience and waved him down, "Sit down!"

"Oh, leave him alone," said Kimmy. "It'd be better to let him play on the expressway and bounce off a Mack truck. Put him out of his misery."

Martha could understand crazy. There was no doubt that Kimmy was crazy; no sane person could say things like that. What Martha couldn't understand was cruelty. How could someone be so cruel?

The towheaded little girl with the tangled hair twirled her umbrella placidly on the porch looking over the head of her older brother, who seemed not to notice anything other than his toy cars. The little girl watched Kimmy and Martha intently, listened to everything.

Oh little girl! Little girl! Martha wanted to whisper in her ear. What will you remember? Who will you become under the influence of such a mother? Will you rise above or sink below her example?

"Isn't that right, old man?" Kimmy said. She pointed at him with the hose and splashed Martha's leg again. Martha hopped back a step, and Kimmy laughed.

"What, are you afraid of a little water?" She flipped the hose again and glanced Martha's other leg with a few drops.

"Stop!" Martha said. Her voice devolved into a full-fledged whine, and she felt reduced to a child again on the playground being teased because she was the only fourth grader fat enough to have breasts that bounced when she skipped rope.

"Stop," Kimmy mocked.

"Kim." Martha's heart bumped against her throat, her larynx constricted. "You stay on your side, and I'll stay on mine. I'm going to ignore you, and I'll ask that you ignore me, and we'll get along just fine."

She pressed the orange button to rev the wacker. Kim had turned her back on Martha, and Martha felt a weak surge of victory, but then Kimmy decided she hadn't had enough fun. She rhythmically flipped the nozzle, each time sending the water close to the wacker, but not on it. Kimmy wiggled her butt in a weird little dance. She was on the verge of laughter.

Martha's face itched with heat. She looked up for a moment at the little girl.

"Too close?" Kimmy said.

Martha tried to ignore her. She moved the wacker as smoothly as possible along the edge, watched the grass clippings and the dirt spew out onto the thin walkway. She tried to keep moving and not flinch when the water splattered close.

"How's that? Huh? What about this? Is that legal distance?"

Finally exasperated, Martha stopped. "Kim, what is your problem?"

Kim looked truly defeated for a moment. Martha thought she'd reached a rational part of her, and that she would even comfort her if Kim began to cry.

"I'm so tired," Kim said. Her shoulders slumped; her expression changed to reveal a person capable of real engagement, with a possibility for complex human inter-action. "You don't know." But as her eyes met Martha's her expression shifted again, and with only a few minor adjustments she traveled the unbelievably short distance between sadness and anger.

"You and your stupid, precious yard, that's my prob-lem." She spoke very slowly, and very clearly. The volume of her voice swelled and shrank erratically. "I have to take care of EVERYTHING myself. All you have to take care of is your YARD. It's not that easy for everyone." She twisted her mouth into an acrid smirk. "Are you going to call the POLICE on me now for watering my lawn?"

"Kim," Martha said shaking her head. "You're not even making sense." She wasn't going to say it, she wasn't, but it came out like a powerful, long suppressed burp, and it felt good: "You're crazy."

She saw that her insult hit home, but in the same instant a momentary look of joy lit Kim's face; the battleground was Kim's home, and she was welcoming Martha to it. Martha perceived her own mistake immediately.

Kim timed her response like a virtuoso. She let a beat pass in which Martha had time to panic, and then said in a slow whisper, "Crazy? Yeah. I'm crazy. Three kids makes me crazy." She smiled calmly. As she continued to speak, her lips snaked through a range of expressions too terrifying for Martha to turn from.

"Busy-body neighbors drive me CRAZY," Kimmy continued. "Living next door to a fat-assed, dried-up VIRGIN who calls the police every time I fart drives me CRAZY."

Kimmy's voice grew more frenzied. She had been in the middle of her lawn at the start of her tirade but had gradually moved step by step closer to Martha, alternately shouting and whispering her words.

"I AM crazy. I'm not like you. I'll never be like you," she hissed. "You're OLD. You're UGLY. You're FAT. You will ALWAYS be ALONE." Neighbors began to appear on porches. Kimmy increased her volume.

"Old virgins go crazy too, ya know. That's what you're really afraid of isn't it? Is that what's going to happen to you? You gonna go crazy, you OLD VIRGIN?"

Kimmy savored the last word, her whole face tensed to spring it with maximum force from her mouth.

"You need a MAN, is what you need. You'll never find a man to fill that DRIED UP OLD HOLE. Squeak! Squeak! Squeak! Isn't that why you're jealous of me? Admit it. All dried up?" With the final taunt, Kimmy's hand twitched, and she pressed her thumb down over the hose's nozzle, forcing the water into a fast stream.

Martha saw the stream, watched Kimmy's elbow bend, as if to lift, as if to aim. Martha blocked her movement with the weedwacker. She hit Kimmy's hand with the metal guard, and it drew blood. Kimmy threw down the hose and came at Martha. Martha stepped back and, in lieu of a growl or a bark, pressed her thumb down on the orange button to rev up the wacker, hoping the noise would be enough to keep Kimmy at bay. At first she held it up in front of her to prevent Kimmy's advance, which it did. The wacker spun between them, two figures momentarily frozen in the impasse of battle, and then Martha gave in to the overwhelming urge, tilted the wacker slightly, aimed at Kimmy's midsection and striped it with welts.

Kimmy backed away with a howl.

Martha moved forward, went for her legs.

Kimmy fell prostrate on the lawn, her screams almost operatic.

Martha found her voice. "Example!" Martha said. And then louder: "Example!" She saw the little girl--wide eyed on the porch--for only a moment, then returned her attention to Kimmy. She lowered the wacker again, this time to Kimmy's thighs. Kimmy jerked and kicked and rolled on the lawn, but Martha followed her. The spinning plastic cord of the wacker striped Kimmy's arms, the backs of her legs, her back.

"Example!" Martha shouted with each application of the wacker. "Example! EXAMPLE!"

She had thought the wacker was relatively harmless, that it would never draw blood, but she found that if she held it in place long enough, at the flesh on the elbow Kimmy raised to protect her face, for example, she did indeed draw blood.

All Martha could utter was "EXAMPLE!" in a voice she didn't recognize, but was satisfying all the same.

Both children hopped up and down on the porch, screamed and cried. Martha's own father howled something as well. Neighbors rushed out into their yards to watch as Martha raised and lowered the wacker, her thumb caressing the orange button. Kimmy writhed under the wacker's touch until, after a while, she merely curled into a ball like a maggot and twitched.

Miss Jackson and Miss Johnson missed most of the action, but on hearing the crying of the children and the inhuman noises Kimmy made, came running out of their house and hopped off their porch. Miss Johnson yanked the extension cord, tore it loose from its plug. The wacker lost its juice, and Martha looked around.

Kimmy lay striped and glowing at Martha's feet, Miss Jackson moved toward Martha with her arms outstretched, but stopped a few feet away.

In the ecstasy of her fury, Martha hadn't noticed that her father had wandered off the porch and was headed down the street. A surge of relief at watching him go complicated her annoyance. The great round earth spun beneath her feet. She curled her toes inside her sneakers as if to hang on, as if all laws were broken and gravity would soon disappoint her too.

When the drone of the wacker subsided in her ears, when her head began to clear and her heart to lift, she saw that half a block away one of the neighbors--an older black man with a pink scar that cut his left eyebrow in two, a man she'd seen before but didn't even know--out of sheer kindness, stopped her father. The man turned her father around gently.

She barely heard Miss Jackson softly repeating, "Martha? Martha? Honey?"

The man didn't have to, of course, but he held her father's hand, both their arms bent at a right angle, the inner sides touching to the elbows, almost like lovers. Martha, her attention riveted on the man and her father, with a flick of her wrist sent the wacker twirling blindly behind her across the lawn and into her bushes. She listened as it hit the dirt with a soft thud, and unclenched her hands. With the whole neighborhood watching, and the sirens whistling in the far distance, this one gentle man walked slowly down the block to lead her father back home into the enduring hollows of Martha's embrace.

EXILES

Grace Quinn sat in the dark kitchen imagining all sorts of horrors. She listened for the water's whistle so she could wet the tea and calm herself as she waited for the sound of Dennis's car pulling over the gravel in the driveway. He'd always been a good boy, and she hoped he still was.

Grace, a small, shapely woman with curves that fell just short of fat, had curly silver-threaded black hair that she most often wore in an upsweep because of its tendency to sprout like stiff wires at all angles if left untamed. Tonight she left it down and let the curls fall where they may. Her Thom thought her a fool to be waiting up for their grown son. She hadn't done so for Colm, the oldest, or Myles, or Iggy, who was a slice of the devil himself, or either of the girls, Eileen and Nora, so why was Dennis different, he wanted to know. But he knew. Dennis was the youngest, and had sprung almost from out of nowhere. Just after Nora was born, Grace had thought the change was coming on her early, but it turned out to be Dennis. She and Thom had just opened the café and bookstore near Wayne State called The Bee-Loud Glade, and yet one more baby wasn't what they were after. The surprise of it nearly knocked her over, and then she'd almost lost him at that. His was a most painful birth, not because he was big—he was just a little bluebird-sized thing—but because he lingered, pounding the insides out of her, refusing to come out until, in the twenty-fifth hour, they finally yanked him out with barely a pulse left for either of them. Although delicate, he'd grown into her most beautiful child with wild black hair and eyes to match, and smooth, pale skin that pearled with high emotion.

It was a curious thing watching your child grow, and then grow up. Watching puberty hit was hard on everyone involved, to be sure. For Grace, it was like watching the sweet child die; it was the first turning away from the mother, and it killed her too, for a little while. She wouldn't want them to be dependant on her for life, but then again, well, yes, she would, if she were honest with herself.

The O'Brien's dog howled, and the gravel rumbled and crunched in the driveway. Grace held her hands around the cup to warm them, and made her face placid. The door jiggled, swished open, and closed. The landing was right off the kitchen, so Dennis saw her straight away.

"Ma. How're you?"

Grace smiled. "Couldn't sleep."

"Not waiting up for me, I hope." He kissed her forehead. He smelled of alcohol and cigarettes. They kept their voices low, so as not to wake the house.

"It's getting on two-thirty," she said, "and you'll have to be getting up in only a couple of hours for work."

He nodded at her cup. "Tea's not likely to help you sleep. Caffeine, and all."

"It's peppermint. Settles the stomach. Did you have fun?"

"Just out dancing with the Ukrainians."

"They seem a bit of a wild bunch. Do they work weekends?"

"Not really. I guess their parents pay for most things. But they're all smart, and they know where to have fun."

"Be careful you don't get used to what you can't keep up."

"Okay, Mother," he said smirking. "Get yourself some sleep." He smoothed the soft coils at her temples and watched them spring back, and as he turned to go up to bed, she couldn't resist a parting shot.

"Dennis." He turned. "I'm glad you're not a mangled bloody mess sprawled desolate at the side of the road somewhere as I've been sitting here worrying you were. Glad you're home safe."

He walked back, knelt beside her, rested his head in the hollow of her shoulder, and squeezed her in a tight hug. They both laughed, and kissed, and off he went to bed.

When she creaked into bed next to Thom, he said, "All's well, Mother?"

She prodded her cold foot between his warm calves, and laughed. "All's well, Father."

All her other children had had broken bones, semi-serious accidents, and illnesses that could have gone either way. All had recovered, and seemed stronger as a result. Dennis had never had any of that. He was quick, and watchful, and often silent; he managed to avoid the growing pains the other kids barreled through, and because of this Grace feared for him, as if he were delicate crystal on a shaky shelf, or a rare jewel left unguarded. When he started talking about the Ukrainian girl, Grace felt the tremor underfoot; she saw the thief lurking in the shadows.

Her name was Marta. From what Dennis had let drop, she was accomplished enough to become a classical pianist, but she planned to go to medical school. Dennis wanted to be a teacher. He'd first mentioned her as one of a group, but by the time he'd mentioned her by name for the third time Grace knew that there was nothing for it except to have her over for dinner.

Marta was a small girl, delicate, but strong looking with a stern bearing like a dancer, and in this much she seemed a good enough match for Dennis. She had pale red hair, plain brown eyes, a sharp little nose and chin, and, as far as Grace could tell, no sense of humor. Grace stood to greet them when they walked in the front door. She hugged and kissed the girl, as she did with all guests in her home, and Marta immediately stiffened. As soon as Grace released her from the embrace, the girl moved off and behind Dennis's elbow. She looked at Grace and then quickly at every stick of furniture, taking in the layout of the room. Usually people offered a compliment on seeing the thick, white throw on the back of the couch with the Aran pattern that Grace had knit herself, or the bog oak rocking chair, or the Celtic knot rug. Marta said nothing. They followed her into the kitchen to help break ice for the beer bucket in the backyard, while Grace blathered on about some nonsense. She hardly knew what she said, the girl made her so nervous.

Thom had fired up the barbecue in the backyard, and everyone sat in lawn chairs and at the picnic table. Grace had made extra batches of wild honey scones and other specialties from The Bee-Loud Glade. Marta sat in a lawn chair with her back rigid, not touching the back of the chair. She appeared to be making herself uncomfortable on purpose. Grace said, "Dennis, get this girl a better chair. She'll never be able to move again, sitting in that stiff thing."

Dennis said, "It's not the chair, it's her. The Alexander Technique. It's a way of holding the body to optimize performance. It helps her with piano."

"It helps with everything," Marta said. "It gets rid of inefficient habits of movement and accumulated tension."

"But are you comfortable?" Grace asked.

Marta laughed a mirthless little laugh and dismissed Grace's question with a blink of her thick-lidded eyes.

"Would you like some lemonade?" Grace offered. "Fresh squeezed."

"How cute," said Marta, accepting the glass.

Once engaged, Marta talked at length about being Ukrainian. She spoke fervently about how her great-grandparents escaped from Ukraine during what she called The Holodomor, which she explained was Stalin's strategy to starve to death the entire Ukrainian population in 1932 and 1933. Her great-grandparents had gotten out just in time, living as exiles in Norway before moving to the Unites States.

"Ireland had a famine too, no?" she said to Grace. "So you were also exiles."

"No," said Grace. "Our people seemed to have survived all that. My family, and Thom's family too, both came over much later through Nova Scotia. I don't know why they left. I guess just better opportunities."

Marta widened her eyes in surprise. Her nostrils flared, and her head flicked back a notch. The fact that Grace's family "moved" rather than having been exiled seemed to visibly lower Marta's esteem for them. The girl spoke of her ancestors' suffering as an intimate wound, and yet she'd also said they'd died well before she was born.

"Can you be called an 'exile,'" Grace asked, "if you leave of your own accord?" She was just making conversation. She'd have never asked had she known the can of worms it'd open.

Improbable as it seemed, Marta's spine stiffened more as she spoke. "Do you call the choice between staying to starve to death, or leaving to save your life, of your own accord? Do you think watching all your family and friends die one by one by one is a choice?"

Yes, thought Grace, horrible things happen all throughout history: to Christians, Muslims, Jews, Syrians, Armenians, Palestinians, Africans, Native Americans, Chinese, Japanese, Koreans, Serbs, and Croats, and on and on in every nation all over the globe, and it will never stop. But beautiful things happen, too. Marta's great-grandparents lived! They got away and prospered! Their great-granddaughter sat among all the comforts of the modern world soaking up the attentions of a handsome boy! It all depended on how you told your story.

She recognized in Marta the righteous indignation of a studious pupil of indoctrination. But you can't tell people like that anything once they're on a roll, especially if it's a matter of "our people." Everyone has people called "our people."

"Sure, the world is full of atrocities," Grace said to be conciliatory. "You seem to have suffered a great deal." She tilted her head slightly to appear thoughtful, and thought, especially for something that happened eighty years ago to someone you never even met. She refrained from pointing out that those left behind had it hardest. She didn't mention that she thought it a sin not to savor every joy that comes your way in this short life. The conversation closed with a snap, and Thom served up the grilled chicken kabobs.

Grace, having noticed the way Marta's consonants slammed out of her mouth, asked if she spoke Ukrainian. Marta said English was her second language, having grown up in the insulated Ukrainian communities of Hamtramck and Warren, and educated in exclusively Ukrainian schools there.

"Almost like us, here in Corktown," Grace said. "Although a lot of the Irish have moved out to the suburbs, now."

"Along with three quarters of the rest of the city," Dennis added.

Grace blinked and went on, telling the girl how she and Thom had both grown up in the Irish section of Bad Axe, in the Northern part of Michigan's thumb, before marrying and moving down to Detroit. Marta barely pretended to listen, and Grace got the impression the girl either didn't believe her, or didn't think Grace was as Irish as Marta was Ukrainian, as if it were a contest of some sort. Grace had never, until now, felt not Irish enough, or more generically American.

Having a stranger to dinner was different up north, where people behaved as guests upon entering a foreign community. Down here in the city, there were so many different kinds of communities. Nobody seemed to pay attention to the rules.

The evening was comfortably mild, the barbecue was sizzling, and everyone had something to say. Dennis had just done a cutting impression of Grace's brother, who they called "Weeping Will," a family favorite who grew maudlin and misty when drunk, usually spilling another juicy family secret or two in the process.

"You should talk," said Marta. "You were crying the first time I met you." This comment drew Grace's attention from Eileen and Nora, who were trying to remember if the last secret their uncle had revealed was the accidental pregnancy of one of his many girl-friends, or the revelation that their prettiest cousin got caught shoplifting.

"I was," Dennis said to Marta. He saw that Grace's sudden attention required an explanation.

"I'd just discovered Cheever. I'd read one story a day as a treat to myself. I was sitting in the Pedestrian Mall reading one about an American woman living in Europe." He turned his attention back to Marta. "It's an imperfect story, but it has this one moment. She meets another American and the sound of his voice reminds her of her youth standing by railroad tracks watching a string of trains go by, enthralled with the sounds of the odd names of cities written on the sides of the trains. He lists the cities one by one, names with no apparent musicality, but the string of them together created this kind of spell on me, and then he ends with "clackety clack and out of sight." It just killed me. And then I heard your voice, and looked up, and there you were with Bohdanna and Vera, and they introduced us."

"I thought you were gay or something. Crying over a story."

"But you don't think that now," he said leaning toward her slightly. His smile closed the space between them with an intimacy that curdled the marrow right up Grace's spine.

"No. But I still think you're a little weird. Stories aren't real."

Grace had a trick of letting the muscles in her face relax so that strangers wouldn't be able to detect anything wrong. Her face was calm and passive in a way that appeared inquisitive. Had Dennis looked at her then, he would have known something was wrong, but his eyes were all for Marta. Had he looked at his mother, he might have caught the spirit of her thoughts, if not the particulars: that a girl like that, with no sense of humor, no imagination, no natural human feeling, could only be trouble.

Marta stood up abruptly. "This lemonade needs more ice." She stood in the center of the backyard commanding attention with her slight, girlish figure. "Do you want ice, Dennis?"

He smiled, handed his glass up to her.

"Anyone else? Should I bring out a whole tray?"

Grace stood too. "Sure, there's no need for that, girl. Let me get it for you."

Marta dismissed her with a flick of her hand and turned. "I saw where you keep it. I won't be a minute," and off she pranced.

Grace sat as if she'd been struck. The thought of that girl rooting around in her own house enraged Grace, but she didn't want to show it. She could get up and follow her into the house and have it out, but that seemed rash and unnecessary, so she simply said, "Dennis, go and help her."

He sprang up, almost flying into the house, and Grace tallied up another point for the girl.

Eileen raised an eyebrow, and Nora shook her head as they both looked to Grace. So, she hadn't imagined it after all.

"She says she likes you," Dennis said the following afternoon. Grace had just brought up the last batch of Irish soda bread from the convection oven in the basement, and was getting it ready for Nora to load into the van to take to the Bee-Loud Glade.

"Did she offer that, or did you ask?"

"Jesus Joe, Ma, what difference does it make? She said she liked you, isn't that enough?"

"I've loads of people who like me, Dennis. I'm not desperate for more. That she likes you well enough is all that worries me."

"Well enough," he repeated, and laughed a mocking laugh. She'd heard this laugh when Dennis dealt with his brothers or sisters, but he'd never before applied it to her.

Dennis sat at the kitchen table. Grace had just put a tea bag in her cup and was waiting for the kettle to whistle. She walked over to Dennis, ran her fingers lightly through his wild black hair, and kissed his forehead. "I'm glad you feel comfortable bringing girls home here." He smiled, crooked his arm around her waist, and rested his head against her ribs. The kettle whistled. Grace moved off to make the tea, and said, "You should bring more girls over."

"More girls? Do you think I have a harem?"

"You could though," she said. "But that's not what I want for you either. That was Iggy's way of course, but in the end he's too excitable to handle the mess of it. You're more steady and sensible. Have your fun, is all I'm saying. Don't stop at the first girl that'll let you have your way with her. Shop around."

"Okay," he said with a scalding calm in his voice. "I get your point. There's no need to be a bitch about it."

"Ah, what a little man y'are now, who can spew filth from his tongue at his mother. Is that the way the Ukrainians do? Tearing the heart out of the only people in the world who've given up everything for you? I suppose it's my fault you're the coddled little pup you turned out to be."

"Give ME up, why don't you. Jesus God, woman." Again he used that deathly quiet voice, as if he were too disgusted to bother shouting. But what volume his voice lacked, he more than made up for on his way out.

The slam of the door set the blood beating into her ears, and she knew she'd won a small point, but that the girl had gained the larger point.

"I've made a hash of it with Dennis," she told Thom later that night in bed. He was a short, lean, powerful man with hands like hams and ears like wings laid tame against the sides of his head. He was quick to laugh and slow to talk, but when he spoke, it was as if he'd been gathering his words for a long time. Thom only looked at her when she told him about the argument. He nodded once, and she knew then Dennis had already told him all about it, and that Thom had aligned himself with his son. "It's just growing pains," he finally said, and because he didn't look at her when he said it, she wasn't sure if he meant Dennis, or her.

When he was at home, which he wasn't much over the next week, Dennis skulked in and out, skipping dinner "to study," he said, for his summer classes. In one fly past the fruit bowl, he swooped down for a peach, and Grace cornered him.

"Go on, Dennis, take at least two if you won't be staying for dinner."

He shot a dark, questioning glance at her, and she said, "Now, how long are you going to limp around me like a wounded lion?"

"I thought it was a coddled pup," he said.

She threw her head back and laughed. "Ah, so it is." She corralled him between a chair and a wall, tickled her fingers along his rib cage mewling, "coddle coddle coddle," until he fell away in laughter.

"Stop!"

She held him firmly by the edge of his tee shirt, at his waist. This boy had never had an ounce of fat on him, and with his shirt pulled tight against his body she noticed the broadness of his back, shoulders and chest, like a real man's, over the waspish waist, and felt a pulse of what this Marta girl wanted with him. "I only want you to be happy, Dennis. And, of course, I want to be happy too. But I can't be happy unless you're with someone who makes you happy."

"What makes you think she won't?"

The future tense threw Grace. She'd been talking about now, and she suddenly realized there was real danger here. She had to plan carefully.

"But we don't even know her yet. Bring her back over. Didn't we treat her fine when she was here?"

He looked at her a little doubtfully, and she turned away to find something in the sink to attend to. "It's good to meet strangers," she said. "Have her next week Sunday. For Eileen's birthday."

The Quinns were large in number, slight in stature and build, with an outsized sense of party, even if it was only themselves and a few outsiders. Those outsiders invited in left feeling that to love and fight as intensely as the Quinns was a wonderful thing, the only way to really live. Eileen's striking dark hair and deep blue eyes more than made up for her weak chin and sharp little nose. Her figure was splendid with her long, thin waist and legs, smallish breasts, and nicely curved breeder's hips. Nora was prettier, in a simpler way: small and shapely like her mother, but tight and athletic, with burnt ginger-snap colored hair and copper eyes like Thom's side. She was a star swimmer in high school, and of all the kids she was the only one of them who'd kept up the Irish dancing at the Gaelic League, winning several dance competitions. That summer she and two other girls from the dance troupe swam across Lake St. Clair to raise money for the new soup kitchen the Gaelic League had started. All the Quinns were do-ers.

Their house sat in the middle of a long residential block in Corktown. They had no trees in their yard, but the big oak in the Flannery's yard to the north, and the huge maple in the Casal's to the south gave the Quinns what they felt was the perfect proportion of sun and shade all through the day and evening. The flowers that lined the sides of the fences grew lush, and the watermelon, corn, and other produce in the garden were sweet and juicy.

Grace had shepherded the romances of two of the older boys before, but Dennis was different. Colm, the oldest, was a priestly loner who'd never dated, and probably never would. He was like so many of Grace's single uncles who lived their whole lives in a solitary existence and seemed quite happy. Iggy, the second boy, was wild and lusty until he finally met his wild, lusty match in Imogene. Imogene smoked too much, but never around Grace, and she held her liquor well. Myles fell somewhere between the witty loner, Colm, and fun-loving, incautious Iggy. He married a smart Brazilian girl named Gabriella who, thank god, was lively and funny.

Everyone else had arrived, when Marta entered with Dennis on her arm. She came bearing a bottle of wine, a birthday gift, and two friends. She'd made bracelets in a traditional Ukrainian style with beads of different sizes and colors; one for Eileen, and one for Grace, but nothing for Nora. Nora clearly wasn't bothered, but Grace thought it bad form. In her estimation, Marta would have been better to bring just the one for Eileen's birthday, and kept her transparent attempt at buttering up to herself.

Nora said, "Dennis makes bracelets, too. He does the Celtic knot thing with leather. See the one he's wearing?"

"She has one," Dennis said.

"Have you?"

"It's hanging in my car off the rear view mirror. It's a little too Heavy Metal looking for me."

"Oh!" said Gabriela, looking at her own wristband. "I never think of this. This is super." She strummed a few licks of air guitar, whipped her long hair to and fro, kicked out a leg to land in a crouch, and everyone applauded.

"If you'd like," Myles said to Gabriela, "I could catch a sparrow for you to bite the head off of."

"No, thank you," Gabriela said. "It would spoil my dinner."

Colm lightly slapped his palm against his forehead. "I totally forgot to pick up the sparrow burgers on the way here. We'll have to settle for steak."

Imogene, who wore three of Dennis's leather bands around her left ankle, crossed her leg, dangled her flip flop back and forth, and burped open another can of beer.

During this exchange, Grace had a chance to assess some of the girl's appeal, trying to see how what she found distasteful was an attraction for Dennis. Marta's large-lidded eyes looked disdainful to Grace, but Dennis may have seen them as "sleepy." It seemed to Grace as if it were a great bother to Marta to open her eyes fully, to pay anything real attention, but if she did open her eyes wide enough to look at you, you'd be grateful.

Her two friends were as different from Marta and from each other as two girls could be. The one named Bohdanna was quick and light and full of questions, and when anyone talked to her, she really listened. The politeness that Grace found stiff and pretentious in Marta seemed natural and charming in Bohdanna. The other one, Vera, was happy and cheerful to a fault, and Grace thought her pleasant enough, if a bit vacant. All were unmistakably fashionable, and clearly well-off.

To demonstrate a truce for Dennis's sake, Grace asked Marta, "What kind of doctor do you want to be?"

"The kind that makes a ton of money. Beyond that it doesn't make much difference."

"That's a Ukie thing," Bohdanna said. "Our parents beat it into our heads that we have to be successful and respectable, so we're all doctors and lawyers and such when we really want to be poets and pianists."

"I never said I wanted to be a pianist," Marta protested with a huffing laugh. Even her own witticisms didn't seem to make her happy. "I'd never make any money doing that."

"But you want to be a poet?" Grace asked Vera.

"No. I'm 'and such.' I'm going to be a dentist. And I want to be a dentist. Bohdanna's the poet."

"Yes," said Bohdanna. "But law school first. For the parents. And Dennis says he wants to be a teacher, but I think he should be a writer. He has a long, long way to go, though. But with sufficient attention and application you can never tell. He needs to take himself more seriously. As a writer, I mean. He needs to take himself a little less seriously, otherwise."

"Teacher, writer, whatever," said Marta. "Our parents aren't stupid. Dennis should take himself more seriously, not less." She turned to Dennis. "I don't know why you don't go to law school."

"Because I don't want to be a lawyer."

"You may not be smart enough anyway, but you could at least try."

Bohdanna unleashed a cudgel of Ukrainian on Marta. Marta huffed another scoff-filled laugh, and although she appeared to have been scolded, she seemed to take it as a compliment. Vera looked nervously back and forth between them. Dennis couldn't have possibly understood their language, but he seemed to understand the intent. He touched Bohdanna's and Marta's arms, and said, "It's okay. That's what I like about her. I love honest people."

If Grace were being honest, she would have said, You can be honest without being nasty. A lot of people mistake cruelty for honesty. But she held her tongue, and caught Dennis's eye. He looked away quickly, and she was satisfied. Then the girl briefly reached for his hand, squeezed lightly, let go, and Dennis beamed.

There is meanness and hardness of heart, but when pheromones circle around a boy the cloud of desire becomes stronger than the substance beneath the cloud. Many a ship has sunk this way. Grace saw that this girl thought she was too good for Dennis, and she wasn't afraid to let him know it. There was no way of telling which way it would go. She might use him and dump him for someone she thought more worthy, or she might shackle him and trounce him under foot for the rest of his life.

"It's a scalding kind of life to work at a job you don't love," Grace said. She'd directed her comment to the girl, but it was Dennis who responded.

"Actually," he said, "I'm thinking of grad school."

"For English?" Marta huffed.

Perhaps it was a birth defect, Grace thought, that nothing this girl said could come out without sounding like mockery.

"Yes," said Dennis. "You may be able to call me 'doctor' yet."

"Since when?" Grace and Marta said at the same time.

"I finished my teaching credits last year. The more English Lit classes I took, the more I realized this was what I really loved. I've been taking summer classes so I can get French and German minors along with my English major."

Nora asked, "Does Wayne State have a good grad program?"

"It's not the top of my list."

"So, then," said Eileen, "U. of M.?"

"Don't know exactly. I'm going to apply to lots of places. I figured why not go big. Maybe Harvard. Maybe Oxford. Maybe University College Dublin."

Grace's heart lumped up to her throat, then sank down with a dull thud. "And how do you plan to pay for that?"

"Same way I do now. Scholarships and work."

"Are you applying to these places?" Grace asked Marta.

Marta, slightly flustered, said, "Wayne State and U. of M. both have good medical schools. I guess I should think about other places…" Marta trailed off, looked at Dennis, and waited for him to speak.

"Who knows if I'll get in anywhere. It's very competitive."

Another huff of laughter. "Competitive? It's not like it's medical school. How competitive could English Lit be?"

"Are you crazy, Marta?" Bohdanna asked. "In this economy? It's way easier to get into med school than grad school in the liberal arts these days."

"That's so cool," said Vera. "I've never been to Ireland. If you go there, could we come visit you? That would be so cool."

"You'd leave home?" Thom said, holding Grace's hand.

Dennis said, "It'd be a mighty commute, wouldn't it?"

Grace had never imagined the rest of her life without Dennis near her, and she couldn't believe that he'd imagined his life away from her. Grace now saw that the first part of her life was over. She shook her head quickly as if shooing away a fly that had flown too close to her eyes, and Dennis went on.

"Detroit is dead. Hundreds of thousands of houses abandoned. More than half the street lights in the city don't work. Over an hour for the police or fire department to respond, if they respond at all."

"But not here in Corktown," Grace said.

"Our neighborhood is just lucky. For now. Close enough to downtown to matter, organized and with just enough money to keep things running, mostly at our own expense. Poorer neighborhoods and mostly black neighborhoods aren't as lucky as we are. You know that."

"You'd go away from us, Dennis? Easy as that?"

"The Chinese are buying up all the empty houses for the land. Everyone here will be pushed out. Before you know it Corktown'll be Shanghaiville. The Russians, Saudis, and Chinese are all hovering around right now waiting to buy up all the art in the Detroit Institue of Arts."

Grace shook her head again. "That'll never happen. That's not true."

"Look around you, Ma. Detroit's an abandoned, bankrupt shit hole. There's nothing here. And anyway, wouldn't it be great if I were to go to Ireland? You're always on about how Irish we are all the way back on both sides, but none of us has ever even been there. We were all born here. Nobody's been back since Gram and Pa came over when they were babies. Wouldn't you like to go to Ireland to visit me?"

Detroit's decay had nothing to do with it. Dennis was only trying to impress this girl, to make her see him as worldly. Grace was sure of it. A mother spends her whole life doing the best for her kids, trying to keep them out of the grips of dangerous strangers, and in this, too, she'd failed. She could keep her peace no longer.

"I've no desire to go anywhere, Dennis. Everything I have that means anything to me is right here. I live here, whatever its troubles, and so do you. Why go traipsing all over the world when we've many fine colleges right here in Michigan? Everyone who loves you is here."

"Well. As I said, nothing has happened yet. I don't start applying until the fall."

"And what about all your pretty little friends?" She waved an open, upturned palm toward Bohdanna, Vera, and Marta. "You'd leave them all behind you, too?"

Marta didn't utter a word until Grace pressed the point. "And what do you think about this? If Dennis went away to England or Ireland?"

Marta drew together her coldest manner and laughed another of her mirthless laughs. "He's a big boy. He can do what he likes. It has nothing to do with me."

Dennis listened with interest, and kept watching her even after she finished speaking, but she wouldn't look at him. In the silence that grew after she spoke, Marta collected the emptied paper plates leisurely, half absent-mindedly, carrying them over to the plastic garbage pails set against the garage. On the trip back to her lawn chair, she stopped to survey the gladiolas at the edge of the fence, and then the rest of the garden. She stood next to her chair, and said to Grace and Thom, "Which of you is the gardener?"

"It's Nora, actually," said Thom.

"Well done Nora." She nodded and smiled at Nora, and looked dreamily at the garden, speaking to no one in particular. "Growing corn in the city. It's a miracle, no?"

Of course, there was nothing miraculous about it. It was only natural. Corn will grow anywhere there's the right combination of sun and water and good dirt, but the fact that the girl could see the miraculous in the mundane threw her into a completely different light for Grace.

A plane sounded faintly overhead, and Grace looked up to spot it. Their backyard was smack under the landing lane for the Detroit Metro Airport. Dozens of planes flew overhead every day, some so high up that only long vapor trails marked their paths, some low and droning, like this one. Grace had heard of birds getting sucked in and pulverized by jets, clogging up engines, bringing planes down. It was a wonder you didn't hear stories of them dropping out of the sky every day of the week.

It wouldn't be accurate, or even fair, to say that Grace had hoped the break-up would have been more dramatic. She wasn't with them when Dennis and Marta broke it off a month after the backyard party, so she'd never know. At one point she'd have asked Dennis about anything that had happened in his life. At one point he'd have told her everything down to the last wrenching detail, but that Dennis and that Grace were gone. Some sort of barrier had sealed off tiny bits of his life to her labeled 'none of her business.' The new Dennis could take or leave what he wanted, even her. Autumn came, school started again. Imperfectly printed pages from application forms to

English and Irish schools appeared in the wastebasket by the family's printer in the den.

All that was left of the break-up for Grace was an abbreviated re-telling of the barest facts when she asked about Marta.

"Oh. No," said Dennis. "That's all over."

It was late, around eleven o'clock. They were the last two up. She sat in her rocking chair reading a book. He sat on the couch braiding together slim strips of leather to make another wrist band.

"Are you sad?" she asked. And here is where hope rose up unwanted, like a hungry, ill-bred dog looking for scraps. To be able to comfort her boy, her favorite boy once more, would be like a gift. Who knew if another chance would ever come along. She wanted to pet him, to soothe him, to work the magic of mother on child. She wanted to weave the spell that would bloom in him later in life when he most needed it and least expected it. No matter how far he traveled from her, no matter how long they might go without seeing each other's faces, they would always be connected. She wanted her boy to understand that to the end of his days—even when he'd become a man, even after his mother had long crumbled to dust—that he was loved, purely and simply. She wanted to be sure he knew it even more so after he'd loved and won, or loved and lost, many women. She knew hers was a different kind of love, but no less powerful for all its difference, because there was something the same about it, too.

And right then, she wanted just one teardrop to wipe from his cheek. But Dennis waved her off. With the ends of the leather strips dangling, he tried to sweep the whole thing away as so much nothing.

"She's a little too smart for me."

"Ah," Grace said. She was going to leave it at that and return to her book, letting him slip off into his own life, as his own man, leaving his mother far behind, as was only natural. It was true, what Dennis had said. Detroit was no place for the young and vibrant. The city had emptied out, but in the abandoned neighborhoods one now saw pheasants, goldfinches, even scarlet tanagers among the wildflowers and vast fields, the likes of which Grace hadn't seen since she lived in the farmlands up north. Despite the desolation, she couldn't help but feel a certain fascination with nature's swift, wild reclamation of the land. The stars at night were brighter without all the streetlights, the crickets louder in the absence of traffic. But this new quiet beauty wouldn't last either.

Dennis tugged together the last bits of leather on the wrist band. Grace set down her book down, moved over to the couch, wrapped her arms around him, and kissed his forehead. Little man though he was, he fell into her hug and rested there. After a few moments he shifted to free himself, but she held him fast just a little while longer before letting him slip off to bed while she turned off the lights, and locked all the doors.

THE COLLECTOR

The ping of aluminum stretching under the sun rang off the roofs in Boue Rouge Trailer Park. Light sparked off windshields, and heat squirmed the air above the tar lots where I'd spent another afternoon collecting discarded beer and soda pop bottles and cans. My Huffy bike sported a metal rack on the back and a basket in front where I strapped canvas bags filled with returnables. Between foraging trips, I stored my loot in a three and a half wheeled grocery cart hidden behind a thatch of bushes that grew between the back entrances of the B&O Bar and Xpressions. That summer Detroit sweltered under a low-lying blanket of cloud and mist. I'd gotten used to sweat tickling its way down my sides and off my eyebrows as I went about my rounds, but when the sun suddenly broke through at the end of the summer, stirring white heat in with the humidity, it made me ornery.

I trawled the long grasses of fields, the edges of empty lots, and the garbage bins near the gas stations lining the service drive to I-96, and I'd hauled in a jackpot. I chained my bike to a metal sign sunk into the concrete behind Xpressions that read: "Parking for Delivery Trucks ONLY. VIOLATORS WILL BE TOWED," which everybody ignored. All the cars belonged to the men who skulked into Xpressions. Some waited to go in if another man had just parked, some looked around warily as they stepped out of their cars, and some had a focus of purpose so clear that they never looked at anyone or anything as they skirted briskly inside. A man, dressed in a jacket and tie despite the heat, had just gotten out of his car and stopped dead hearing the clatter of my cart. He kept his eye on me while I rinsed cans at the faucet behind the B&O, and when he thought I wasn't looking, he disappeared into Xpressions, the purple door yawning closed behind him. In lower, weaker moods, I capitalized on such seclusion to root through the dumpster for discarded porn. That day I resisted the urge, finished rinsing the returnables, and limped my cart to the Seven-Eleven to cash in.

A few years earlier, my mother had inherited a mobile home from her Uncle Eugene. We already lived in a trailer, so Mom enlisted Sister Hildegard, the shop teacher at Saint Benedict's, to help gut the mobile home and turn it into something useful. Sister Hildegard pinned her wimple up into a knot on her head to keep her broad neck cool in the summer heat while she and some of the other Sisters transformed Uncle Eugene's bachelor pad into a Bookmobile, which Father Pastula let us keep in Saint Benedict's parking lot. Church donation drives filled fewer than a quarter of the shelves, so I decided to help by donating the money from the returnables to buy used books.

For a few hours every afternoon, Mom drove the Bookmobile into the worst neighborhoods in Detroit, and parked. On one side of the Bookmobile Sister Immaculata, the art teacher, had painted a picture of a man with an open book in his lap, and a woman leading a group of people toward the man. The man looked like a dark brown version of Abe Lincoln with a lopsided afro. Sister Immaculata painted "Frederick Douglass" and "Harriet Tubman" in neat cursive letters under the man and woman, and above them she printed "People's Library." The Bookmobile hulked through the projects, parked, and opened its doors, where a thin white lady—my mother—sat and waited for patrons. Her deep widow's peak, which went gray long before any other part of her black hair, gave her a look both magisterial and spooky. She struggled with the Bookmobile's large steering wheel, her arms braceleted with rubber bands, and drove to the areas of least hope, where drugs, alcohol, and lottery tickets were easier to get than books. About a quarter of the books were not returned, but my father joked that if they didn't return the books to her they'd return them to him. He was the librarian at the Detroit House of Corrections. At first, he'd insisted on accompanying Mom, but they shortly agreed that she needed to do her own thing. So, while Mom was parked in the projects, after work Dad jumped rope, and did push-ups outside on the patio he'd built beside our trailer. The worse the weather, the better he seemed to like it, and if one of the neighbors told him he was crazy, he'd smile, shrug with elbows bent and palms up, and then start jumping.

I appeased Dad for a while by accompanying Mom at the beginning, but I found it achingly boring. Instead, I devoted my energies to the funding of books with my returnables, and the whole family was happy: Dad jumped rope, Mom served the disadvantaged, I collected cans, and Janey stayed busy being Janey, working elegant solutions to complex mathematical problems of her own design on the back of old cereal boxes while singing along with the radio.

Janey's classmate, Denis L'Heureux, worked the one to nine shift at the Seven-Eleven. Janey'd tutored him in calculus, then helped him study for the SATs. In return he helped her learn French, because Janey hadn't had a spot in her schedule for French. Among their other ideas about our development, our parents felt it best to keep Janey's double promotions down to three. Although she was two years younger than I, Janey was a senior while I was a junior. Our parents felt being with students closer to her own age would be better for Janey, socially. But as a result, she was heavy bored. School wouldn't allow her to take more than seven classes a semester, so she quenched most of her curiosity with advanced math books, and side projects like French with Denis.

Janey memorized all the vocabulary, verb tenses, gendered nouns, and attendant rules within a week, but her spoken French was horrific, and this is where Denis was useful because he spoke French at home. This was how we learned that Boue Rouge meant red mud, that Denis' name was not spelled "Denny," like the restaurant, and that we'd been mispronouncing it, too. They studied together in what we called the "doghouse," even though we'd never owned a dog. In place of the simple tent I'd set up one year beside our trailer, Janey conceived of the doghouse, complete with a way to rain-proof and ventilate it using wood slats and aluminum siding we stole from the junkyard that abutted our trailer park.

Three o'clock was a slow time at the Seven-Eleven. Denis leaned on the counter, one arm raised, fly swatter in hand. He focused on a large fly that had settled, when I rattled in with my first bag of empties, startling the fly.

"Damn Thomas," he said, in a way that made it sound as if Damn was my first name. "I've been chasing that fly for days. I was this close." He pinched his thumb and forefinger about a fly's width apart.

"Yeah," I said. I ignored the convoy of flies that trailed the sweet and sour muck stuck to my bag. "Sorry. You want to count with me?"

"No," he said. "Just keep quiet. Maybe I can get that fly." As I rumbled through the swinging doors to the back room he yelled, "They clean?"

"What do you think?" I said.

Denis kept himself busy with the fly while I carted and counted the returnables, stacking them neatly in wooden crates that lined one wall of the pungent back room. On my last trip he said, "Need help?" He flicked his head this way and that, and his straight, dark hair flopped about accordingly, always somehow managing to end up back in his eyes, not quite covering them.

"Nope. Last trip," I said. He gave up on the fly, settled back on the counter with his book of crossword puzzles.

By the time I finished I was sticky all over, despite the portable fan in the corner that blew hot air from one spot to the next. I sat on an empty crate, lifted my shirt and aimed the fan at my newly trim belly, for which I thanked myself and Simone Weil, my new hero. She'd written that she starved herself in sympathy for the Jews in the Nazi concentration camps. Born into a wealthy Jewish family in France, she too had grown up with somewhat eccentric parents, and she too had had a sibling of abnormal genius. Saint Francis and Saint Theresa with their dogged humility were too holy to remain role models for me, and I could no longer buy the hocus pocus of stigmata and rose-scented corpses. I chose the secular Simone as my guide, although I acknowledged that she went crazy at the end and became, among other things, a self-loathing, Jewish anti-Semite, and a raging, manipulative anorexic. As we tend to do with heroes, I blotted out her more disgusting aspects, and focused on the qualities I admired: her early days of rigorous self-abnegation, which served as an example that spurred me to lose the fifty pounds of hot-dogs and donuts I'd acquired through my Catholic school days. If ever I suffered from hunger or inconvenience, I thought of Simone Weil and her sacrifices, and of people who were far worse off than I. Simone went crazy, but it was exactly because her ideas of social justice and moral purity mingled with her own human failures, because she was so clearly faulty, so obviously far from perfection, that I felt a special kinship.

I peeked out front: a trucker bought cigarettes; a fat woman in a pink halter-top with three fat kids in tow covered the counter with five varieties of chips and an eight pack of Mountain Dew. I waited until everyone left before I went out to collect my bounty of twelve dollars and thirty-five cents. Denis paid out, then sat back on the ledge behind him, one foot on the checkout counter, an elbow propped on his upraised knee.

"How's Janey?"

"Fine, I guess." I leaned my hip against the counter. "Math camp."

"Yeah? Where? For how long?"

"Cranbrook. Comes home this weekend."

"Cool," he said.

I nodded. I was happy someone like Denis appreciated Janey as much as I did.

"It is cool, isn't it," I finally said.

He knit his brows as if it were ridiculous to say something so obvious. "Very." Then after a pause he added, "Your whole family is cool."

I flicked out my elbow. He flicked back his hair.

"Too bad she's not around, I was going to ask you guys over. Anyway, you could come alone if you want to go swimming," he said. "It's just a little four footer, but…"

"That'd be cool."

He flicked back his hair, bounced the rolled-up paper off his knee. "You know where I live?"

I pointed south. "Sort of."

"On Brammell. It's," he started, then thought better of it. "I'm done at nine. Meet me here. Just bring your suit. You can use one of our towels."

I waved goodbye, then clattered back behind Xpressions to park and chain up the cart, veering far from the dumpster to avoid the near occasion of porn.

Riding home I pedaled as if I were running, faster and faster until I thought my heart would burst. Then I sat, glided, and breathed in the bouquet of late summer afternoon: grasshoppers crouching in hot, high grass; water sprinkling lawns; people sweating on porches; lighter fluid, charcoal aflame, hamburger; wild gladiolas and cat piss. Brammell stopped at the service drive to I-96, where a construction project begun in winter had repeatedly stopped and started all through the summer. They'd dug up the vacant fields there, torn down two burnt houses and the gas station at the corner. That summer they transformed the littered wasteland into a weird moonscape with deep, fresh craters and huge dunes of sand and gravel.

Maybe because of the heat or the time of day, the dunes were deserted. I leaned my bike against a light post, stepped off a few paces and ran full speed ahead up the side of the highest dune, but at one point my foot caught, and I sank dangerously low before I twisted my body flat onto the pile, unstuck my leg and rolled down, leaving half the skin of my knee somewhere among the gravel. Just before I got back on my bike, I looked up to see the flattened spot where my leg had sunk. It was the highest mark on the dune. I had had the most successful run and tumble ever, and all I had as witness were the scrapes on my knees and the scar on the dune. I had no way of proving that scar was mine, but then reminded myself that doing something for the eyes of the world was vainglory. Although I had no way to prove it to, say, Denis, I had triumphed, and that should have been enough, even though in my heart of hearts I knew it wasn't.

Dusk came late, and in the last few hours of sun the gray fluff of dandelion gone to seed floated everywhere. Neither Mom nor Dad had yet come home, and Janey wouldn't be back from Math Camp for a few more days. I pushed a chair against the bedroom door, reached under my mattress for the magazines I'd fished from the dumpster behind Xpressions during lapses in judgment earlier in the summer, and spread them flat on the only desk in the room. I propped my oversized "Art of the Western World" upside down with the pages spread away from me so that if an intruder entered too rapidly, I only had to push the magazines forward to make the art book tumble down, face up over the skin mags. I pulled my chair as close as it would go to the desk, turned pages with my left hand, and reached beneath the desk with my right. I dawdled and played, trying to make it last by concentrating on the pictures of naked women, hoping to re-train my brain to normal. I only kept Penthouse, which always had a spread of a couple in different scenarios. At the sight of the horny Robin Hood ravaging Maid Marian, or the athlete in white socks surprised naked by a cheerleader, I forgot to look at the women, and forgot about any desire to be normal. The awareness that I had once again failed to master my lusts increased the titillation. This time the inevitable but ever-surprising shudder and squirt arrived before I'd finished my third pass through the spread. I cleaned up using the wad of toilet paper I'd had the foresight to gather into my fist beforehand.

And then came remorse.

Sleepy, disgusted with my weakness, I fought the urge to doze, pushed away from the desk and looked around the room. This time I would succeed in ridding my life of the dross that clouded my mind and obscured my focus. I regretted the time I'd lost indulging my lusts that could have been better spent reading or drawing. I had to pay. Although chastity is the virtue that counters lust, you can't do chastity after having just masturbated. Charity, however, is a concrete act. Discarding favored possessions felt like a just penance to remind myself to be a better person. Whatever I wanted to keep most should be the first to go. I had failed over and over, but this time I found the strength to throw the magazines away. I prepared one pile with the magazines for the trash, another pile for clothes and other stuff for the Salvation Army. I'd circled around my Rubik's cube on my most recent purges knowing I'd have to get rid of it some day, but hadn't yet found the strength. In its absence, I'd force myself to learn a new skill, or French. I grabbed the blue velvet Crown Royal sack filled with colored stones that I'd collected and polished, a little mirror framed with coiled copper that Janey had made for me, a medal I'd won for a spelling bee, and a ten year old strawberry candle that still smelled good, which Sister Jacqueline had given me when I was her pet. Typically, I worked these purges as quickly as possible to leave no time for doubt or regret. I swept up my possessions in one movement, then tore away breathless on my bike.

I threw the magazines into one of the many dumpsters that lined the entrance to Boue Rouge, choosing these bins for their peculiar filth as a disincentive to keep me from fishing them out again later, as I'd done occasionally in the past. Beyond the mile or so of gas stations, fast food drive-thrus, and auto repair shops, I dumped my favorite things into a covered Salvation Army donation bin, then rode away and tried to feel free.

Once I'd gotten good at purging, I had occasional difficulty remembering what I'd thrown away. Other times sadness came like a storm, sometimes immediately, sometimes late at night as I lay in bed—it was part of the whole experience. Discarding aspects of the material world to which one has become unduly attached was the point. The more I did it, the better I got at it and, as with the other purges, I had faith the quiet riot of my sadness would eventually abate.

I teetered on my bike next to Denis as he walked the five or so blocks to his house. Once inside, Denis' mother and father both rushed to greet him. His father smiled broadly and put his hand tenderly on Denis' shoulder; his mother combed a hank of hair out of his eye with her forefinger. Denis' older sister had gone out with friends, and his younger sister was watching television, so we would have the pool to ourselves. He introduced me as Janey's brother, and told his parents we were going swimming as he kicked off his shoes, then went off to get two towels, leaving me standing with his foreign parents. They had almond skin, black hair and eyes, and they were both short and beautiful, as I imagined every person in France must be. Denis' father looked like a man who would have been happy anywhere in the world.

Denis' mother had furnished their house like no other home in America. All my other friends in Denis' neighborhood had some form of jaundiced carpeting in the living room, which nearly matched the bilious linoleum in the kitchen. I never suspected there were other options until I saw the hard wood floors that lined the L'Heureux's living room and kitchen. Even the colors of their clothes seemed foreign. Mister L'Heureux's blue-green shirt looked like no blue-green I'd ever seen in Kmart or Sears or even T.J. Maxx. The blue and orange scarf tied in a casual knot around Mrs. L'Heureux's throat perfectly accented her brown skirt and the soft pistachio of her sweater, which looked as though it had been knit to fit her trim figure and no other. I'd never seen a woman so elegant, or so out of place. Everything in their house looked like real art. Mrs. L'Heureux saw me looking at one particular print of a hungry cat leering at a slaughtered bird and rabbit splayed next to a silver bowl with scattered fruit.

"They're all reproductions," Denis said.

"Are they French?"

"Mais, non," his mother said.

Denis' father pointed as he spoke. "Miro and Picasso in the dining room, Spanish. Van Gogh, here, Dutch, but this is his Japanese period."

Mrs. L'Heureux piped in, "Also an American. Alexander Calder. But this is in the other room."

Denis shifted from one foot to the other, bored. His mother pointed at the picture she'd caught me looking

at first. "Chardin, yes, is French. Americans find it sometimes…." She hesitated and turned to Denis. "Affreux?"

"Gruesome," Denis said. Then he quickly added,
"We're gonna swim."

His father threaded his arm through his wife's, kissed
her neck. Denis gently cradled his mother's face with
one hand and stroked her ear with his thumb. When
he moved away, her head bent to follow the warmth
of her son's hand, then she straightened and stood
posture-perfect.

Once outside, Denis picked a pair of light blue boxer
trunks off the cyclone fence between his house and the
neighbor's, and we set our towels and his sun-dried
trunks on the picnic table. I pealed off the cutoffs I'd
worn over my swimsuit, and tossed them next to the
towels. Fully night now, a gibbous moon hung low in the
sky. Denis looked left and right into the empty yards, and
in one swift movement his hair flipped up and flopped
down as his shirt came off. Where before he was just a
skinny guy, now I remembered he'd been on the swim
team as I considered his fine, hairless torso. In one more
movement he slipped off his jeans and underwear. To
this day I'm not sure if I gasped out loud or not. Denis
looked like the apparition of a saint, thin and moonlit.
Against the dark night his white skin framed the black
hair of his bush, and in the center hung a beautiful shock
of white.

His foot got caught pulling on his trunks, he stum-
bled; his white center swung and bobbed and jiggled. The
next thing I knew, he'd righted himself, and he seemed
as completely covered as if he were wearing a snowsuit.

In those ten seconds the world tilted irrevocably toward the frightening inclinations of adulthood that Sister Poland had warned about. My puppy dog pure thoughts of Denis growled into a hounding lust.

Denis squirted water into a shallow bucket, swished his feet, stepped on an overturned milk crate and, leveraging his foot on the pool's metal rim, flung himself in.

I didn't know how to hide my sudden erection. Denis plunged under the water, then slowly rose, his hair plastered to his head and down over his eyes. He sputtered water from his mouth, and bobbed across the surface.

"It's nice!" he said. "Not cold at all."

"I might wait a bit," I said. I squished my body against the pool, rested an elbow on the edge, and with my free hand pressed my embarrassment down, trying to push it, if not into submission, at least into hiding.

He stretched himself out, languid, weightless on the water looking up at the moon. When he shifted his head to look at me, the dark water blanketed his body to his toes.

"Get in," he said.

"In a minute," I cupped the water in my hand. "It feels cold."

"What're you, crazy? It's like bath water. Come on." He edged closer, bobbing and gulping, then splashed a skirt of water into my face, and swam away.

It was enough to shrink me sober. I jumped in and reminded myself of my vow that if I couldn't be straight, I wouldn't be anything. If a celibate life was okay for Simone Weil, it was okay for me.

We paddled and splashed for more than an hour, talking about Denis' plans to leave for college in the next couple of weeks, what it was like for me to have a genius younger sister graduating the year ahead of me, and a hundred other nothings. We bounced a beach ball back and forth, and after the fifth or sixth time it bounced out of the pool we let it lie in the dewy grass. When we'd played ourselves out and our fingers had begun to prune, Denis said abruptly, "We'd better get out now. I guess."

My heart plunged. "Okay," I said, trying to sound off-handed and natural.

"Help me make a whirlpool before we get out. I have to vacuum the pool tomorrow." We dawdled another fifteen minutes or so making and unmaking whirlpools, until finally we built a current so strong that when we lifted ourselves from the pool our legs bent and our trunks drooped down past the tops of our rumps.

Brave and pure and no longer hard, I pulled my suit off before Denis, daring myself to keep control. He looked at me and at my body without any embarrassment, and I thought how nice it must be not to have any sexual desires for another man, how simple and uncomplicated life would be. I felt a certain pride in the burden of desire I determined to suppress my entire life, and I was grateful Denis befriended me.

"Thanks," I said, pulling on my shorts.

"Any time." He wrapped the towel around his waist.

The night was humid, but we were fresh from our swim, so he said he'd walk with me home. "I love walking past houses at night," he said. He leaned forward, shook his hair. The muscles in his back, his stomach, around his ribs expanded and contracted. Then he straightened, and caught me watching him. "Just let me put on some shorts." The smile appeared on his face so quickly it startled me. His eyes crinkled at the corners, and I could tell that at sixty or seventy years old those crinkles would become long, deep creases, and would probably be just as attractive.

The towel around his waist pulled taut as he walked back into the house to change. Even the slight clenching and unclenching of his calves caught my breath.

The humid summer had sent the mosquitoes into a breeding frenzy, and they became voracious, especially in the long stretches between streetlights near houses with long, weedy lawns. We walked faster and faster swatting every inch of exposed skin.

"You don't have to suffer through this," I said. "You could just go home."

"No," he said. "Wait. Shh."

He hopped a fence into a dark yard on the corner, took off his shirt, bundled the pilfered tops of ten or twenty marigolds into it, then hopped back over the fence and ran as fast as he could. I followed him on my bike into an alley. "Marigolds repel mosquitoes," he said, and before I knew it he had lifted off my shirt. He laced his fingers with the marigolds, clapped his hands and rubbed me down from stem to stern, during which time I, petrified, tried not to blink or breathe or think or feel, lest something in the middle of my body should stand up and point to my true deviant nature.

When he finished, he said, "I can't believe you were fat. I mean, of course I believe it, because I saw it. But now, you're completely normal." He pulled a tug of skin at my belly. "You look really good."

He threw the pulverized flower tops onto the gravel in the alley, and we threaded my fingers with marigolds.

"Clap once or twice to release the oils. Don't rub too hard or you'll crumple the flowers before you finish." He spread his legs slightly, and lifted his arms.

I tried to get it over with quickly. Pat pat rub, pat pat rub, and I was done.

"Damn Thomas!" he said. "Do it right! I'm getting eaten alive here. Start over."

Naïvely, I had thought my penis was the only organ I needed to ignore in order to be pure, but I learned that my hands were possibly more dangerous. I successfully crossed the bridge of unreality and convinced myself that Denis' body was just finely contoured glass, still warm from the furnace, barely cooled enough not to blister.

"Does this even work?" I said when I got to his neck.

"We'll see."

He scattered the rest of the marigolds, then pulled his shirt on as I balanced on my bike. The plum tree in front of a house halfway up the block had stained the sidewalk purple with rotting fruit. The television inside threw bright flashes against the window and onto the lawn, but didn't keep us from creeping under the tree to pilfer the overripe plums, which burst on touch. The sweet black-red juice dripped down our arms to the elbow and down our chins. We rinsed off the sticky juice at a sprinkler on the corner and continued on our way.

As we approached the dunes, we heard yelps like the sounds of bats flying over fields down by the river. The freeway lights threw long shadows off the dunes, and in those shadows Denis and I nodded our greetings to the other guys. We each made a few vaults with very little success. The dune was easier just after a rain, but that sunny day had loosened the dirt and it crumbled easily under foot. None of us could get enough of a purchase to propel us up more than a few feet. We quit and continued on to Boue Rouge. As we turned, I couldn't resist. I pointed to the scar near the top of the mound. "That was me," I told Denis.

"Sure it was," he said.

"Really. It was. This afternoon." I pointed to my knee. "I was alone, but…"

"Yeah. Sure. And I'd show you mine, but it's hard to see without a helicopter."

I looked at him, then looked away to stare hard at my handlebars. I walked beside my bike. "I dare you to get that high," I muttered.

Denis leaned into my shoulder and pushed me slowly off the sidewalk onto someone's lawn. We walked along in uncomfortable silence, then he said, "I believe you, you know."

"You should," I said matter-of-factly. "Because it's true."

We walked a few more mosquito-haunted blocks to Outer Drive Road, then headed south over the expressway. Just past the railroad tracks we turned into Boue Rouge. Despite being near the river and woods, the trailer park itself had only thin patches of quack grass and dandelions where bugs could breed, and many more street lights to draw the mosquitoes up and away into an inviting halogen nimbus.

As soon as we entered the trailer park I said, "Your parents are so cool."

"Ha!"

"I mean it. Seriously cool." He didn't respond. "You see they're not like anyone else around here, don't you? Their whole style is different. They have class." I took a deep breath. "Which is why you're so cool, I guess."

He stayed quiet for a moment, then said, "They are cool." He looked slightly stunned. "It's weird how you don't realize things until someone points it out. Thanks."

We stood next to the doghouse under a light as strong as any you'd find on a football field. "It's strange," he continued. "I'm leaving in two weeks and it's like the whole world is exploding. In a good way. All at once I see how good things are—stupid stuff like mowing the lawn: that smell, you know?"

I nodded. Even though we'd never had a lawn, I'd smelled it walking past houses with lawns on the way home from school.

"But even my mom and dad. They are great. And Janey, teaching her French, and her teaching me."

We were quiet. I waited.

"Hmph," he said. He tapped his foot on the patio tiles. "Janey says your Dad jumps rope out here."

I nodded. "Yep."

He swatted himself a few times. "I don't think that marigold thing worked."

"I don't know," I said spreading out my arms to see I had very few bites. "It seems to have worked for me."

He swatted himself again. "Can we get away from these bugs?"

I pulled back the tarp at the doghouse entrance, and then the curtain. Four feet high, eight feet long, six feet wide, the doghouse comfortably fit two or three people. Denis stretched out on one of the two sleeping bags, hands folded over his chest. I pulled down the curtain and tarp, lit a hurricane candle, turned on the small fan we had hooked up to the trailer's power supply, then sat on the other sleeping bag.

"You're not bit?" he said.

"Some." I felt for bumps along my arm and at my ankle.

"Man! I am. Feel my arm."

I trailed the tips of my fingers over the soft skin on the inside of his elbow, up the hard apple of his bicep. It was happening again. I shifted to hide my erection and my anger. I had formerly considered self-control my best quality, but my now rebellious body thwarted me at every turn. If I could endure hunger when I had lost the fifty pounds, why couldn't I exercise more mastery over the rest of my body?

"Those marigolds stink," I said. I lifted my hands to my nose and took a few good, long whiffs.

"A little," he said. "You've got a big one there." He reached over and felt the mosquito bite on my neck with a fingertip. It wasn't fair that I should suffer so much from his touch. I was embarrassed for myself, and angry with him for being straight, oblivious, and normal.

"Maybe I didn't marigold that part well enough." He raised himself on one elbow, sniffed my neck. "I don't smell it." I could feel his breath on my shoulder. "Sometimes saliva helps the itch." His slippery tongue circled the bump, then flattened and strafed against it. He pulled back, but I still didn't move. Although I faced straight ahead, I strained my eyes downward to look at him, and that's when he raised his face to mine and kissed me on the lips. It was soft, warm, short, and utterly shocking.

"Sorry," he said immediately. "I always wanted to try that." He wasn't in a panic, but saw that I was. Still, he retracted only a little. "I'm really sorry," he said, and I could see my panic spreading through the tiny space between us, infecting him. He pulled farther away, but kept his balance on one elbow. "It's probably not your thing," he said. Then he sat up entirely. I could see he was figuring out his exit strategy. "Seriously," he said, "I didn't mean anything. I'm really, really sorry."

"Okay!" I said. "Alright already." A frown twitched my eyebrows.

After a long silence, still looking intently at my toes, just as he uncrossed his legs and moved as if to go, I said, "Anything else you want to try?"

In my peripheral vision I saw his head swivel, his hair flip back. He lifted his hand, as if to bless me, then patted my head softly. I still didn't look up. He spread his fingers, ran them through my hair and moved my head so I'd have to look at him.

"Maybe I should go," he said.

I caught him by the wrist, removed his hand from my head. I kissed his palm. When he smiled, I pulled him closer until we sat side by side. He looked me in the eye, said my full name, and his saying it made it beautiful: "Thomas Keane." I kissed him. Previously, I had thought there was a right way and a wrong way, but with Denis, I learned there were many different ways of kissing, and they all seemed right. And then we reached the shocking nub of it, so to speak. His private skin smelled of new earth with an undertone of chlorine. Our fumblings were few but effective, and before long we had a glorious salty mess on our hands, chests, lips and stomachs.

I collapsed next to him.

Sister Poland had been wrong. There was no shame when we finished, only relief. The crickets chirped, our sighs calmed, a far away train hummed closer.

"Thank you," he said. "You don't know. This is like Christmas, my birthday, every gift I've ever been given times a hundred."

"Sure beats tube socks," I said.

"No, really," he said. "Thank you."

Our hands slid together. We caressed and squeezed intermittently, and lay listening to the chirp and hum of the late summer night. "We can't do this again," he said, but he didn't sound particularly sad, or happy, or angry. He turned his body completely toward me, slippery and sticky at the same time. He stroked my cheek, my neck, my ear; he kissed my forehead, my chin, my shoulder.

"Thank you," he said again, quietly.

"You're very welcome!" We both laughed, and quickly grew silent.

"I mean it." Then he said, "Try not to think about it too much. Okay?"

"Okay," I lied.

He sat up, pulled on his clothes, and crawled to the opening. When he pushed up the heavy tarp I could feel the new coolness of the night. In the harsh beam of the streetlight Denis was all dark silhouette. I rested back on my elbows. He extended his hand against the light, and waved goodbye.

I continued to return my bottles, so I saw Denis often over the two weeks before he was to leave for Berkeley. At first we shifted shyly in not-quite-giggly turns away from each other, but only for a few seconds. His ability to relax relaxed me. We were relieved at what we'd done, and even more relieved we'd agreed never to do it again. When Janey came back that weekend I told her only that I'd gone swimming at Denis'. She seemed happy to have closed the circle of friendship between the three of us. Janey was to leave for MIT two weeks from then, the same day Denis would leave for Berkeley. Janey decided that on Denis' last day at the Seven-Eleven, two days before they both left, we'd go there to say goodbye.

At Math Camp Janey had won an abacus for excellence in something or other with polished colored stones that distinguished the values on each row. Her decision to give this to Denis as a going away gift whipped me into a frothy panic.

I remembered Denis' mother mentioning Alexander Calder. I looked him up, and saw that he was most famous for his stabiles, so I spent the next two weeks cutting and bending sections of metal cans into shapes—stars, moons, flowers, swirling spiral whirlpools.

I hammered down and sanded the sharp edges, painted them bright colors. Hour upon hour passed as I looked for ways to fashion a stabile base; days brightened and faded as I strung the shapes along a wire axis to make the damn thing balance and turn with precision until I got it just right. And then, doubt seized me. I'd thought the stabile would show my gratitude to Denis better than words could, but it all seemed too obvious. It felt equivalent to carrying two dozen red roses through the streets to him.

Janey came into our tiny bedroom to get me, where I paced back and forth.

"This is stupid," I pointed to the stabile. "It's ugly."

"It's not ugly. It's elegant and clever."

"It feels childish."

"It's great, Thomas. What's going on? Come on."

"You go," I said. "Go alone. No, that would be weird. Shit!" Every word brought me closer to tears. I could tell I'd scared Janey, because she looked as if she would cry soon, too. She sat next to me without saying anything and simply stroked my arm as I made up my mind not to give it to him.

"I think this may be expensive," Janey said lifting the abacus. "It's from both of us, okay?" I knew he'd never associate a math gift with me, but when we gave it to him, Denis was all embarrassed appreciation.

"Oh!" he said. "I didn't get you anything. This isn't fair."

"It's not a contest, Denis," Janey said in that calm matter-of-fact tone I imagine only she and gurus on mountaintops have. "Obviously our friendship isn't reducible to any object. This is just something to remind you of us. Whenever I speak or hear French, I'll think of you."

Denis looked at me and I looked back, unsure what to do or say. After an awkward moment Denis said, "Well," raised his hands to his forehead and pulled his hair back tight. His tee shirt stretched to accentuate the round disc of his pectoral muscle, a tiny nub of nipple, the delicate architecture of his ribcage. He puffed out his lower lip, exhaled a long sigh, then let his hair cascade down around his face. He shrugged and said, "Thank you." He had told me in the doghouse that what we'd done was a gift to him, so I loaded his words with meaning, tried to tell if he looked at me longer or at Janey when he said it. In the end I couldn't tell.

Janey gave him a kiss. He and I shook hands, then hugged before saying goodbye and good luck.

The night before Janey and Denis were to leave for their separate coasts, Mom, Dad, Janey, and I sat at the Formica table at the front of the trailer eating meatloaf, mashed potatoes, peas, and corn. Janey answered the phone, which had been ringing all day long with people calling to extend their best wishes.

"Oh. Hi!" she said.

We leaned in to concentrate on Janey, who seemed happy and chipper and comfortable with this person, but the "oh" indicated something of a surprise.

"A Cranbrook friend?" Dad said.

"No," I said. "A teacher, I bet. Mister Dyroff?"

Janey put her finger in her ear and hunched forward to stare down at her meatloaf. Mom didn't venture a guess, but screwed her eyes on Janey the way I'd seen her do the first time Janey waded into wave-churned Lake Huron when we were little.

We watched, listening closely for more details, but Janey had stopped talking. Her smile clouded slowly. And then the natural high pink in her face drained to a gray that bordered on green, and although the last week had been cruelly hot and sunny, all warmth left the room. Her expression numbed, then shards of sorrow trembled over her lower lip and cut quickly in a spasm across her face. The color came rushing back in red blotches over her face, neck, her upper arms.

"Thanks for calling," she said. She held the receiver out and away from her, looked at it for a short moment, and hung up. Then she buckled, face in her hands, and wept. When she could speak again, she told us what she'd just been told: Denis had stopped by the dune. Other kids were there. He made it to the top, found a foothold, stood for a moment, then sank rapidly into the middle, a cascade of sand and gravel following. Nobody knew when the ambulance was called or by whom. Despite the frantic digging by every boy there, and then later by the ambulance drivers, it took half an hour, maybe forty-five minutes—no one could be sure—before they recovered his body.

Janey stayed for the funeral, then left for Boston a week after school started.

The danger with objects is our propensity to attach meaning to them. I ripped apart the stabile I'd made Denis, scattered the sections across weed infested lots, into the filthiest dumpsters I could find, skipped them into the river, down sewers. I expanded my territory, rode farther than I'd ever ridden, strewing stars, moons, whirling pools over as much of this wide, insensate earth as I could cover on my silly little bike.

My senior year started. I tried to face every place and situation that might remind me of Denis in order to layer new associations over the old: the Seven-Eleven, the dunes, my bike, any stray bottle or can. This didn't work.

I stopped collecting cans and joined the swim team. This worked for a time. I'd be fine, gliding through cool water, then I'd do a flip turn and think about Denis' hair, how it might have looked the moment the sand gave way, if indeed the flick of his head had destabilized him. I'd think about how I'd dared him to reach the top, about how he'd been unable to breathe under all that sand. I'd stay under water to see if I could know what it was like for him, but of course, eventually I always resurfaced to breathe.

I'd won a scholarship to Boston College, and the following fall I arrived there amid caravans of kids with computers, televisions, mahogany trunks full of clothes, box upon box of books, games, mementos. I carted all my worldly possessions in my backpack: five shirts, three sweaters, two pair of pants, a tie, a winter coat, a summer jacket, a week's worth of socks and underwear. I stowed my clothes in a closet and kept my room almost completely bare, not unlike every apartment I've lived in ever since. It is easier to let things go.

I'm an adult now and have moved beyond all this, mostly. It doesn't matter, it doesn't matter now, I know that. My aversion to objects and possessions has hardened into habit. I keep the physical world in check as much as possible. I have nothing material left from those days of tin moons and stars, but not all belongings are tangible; some creep into my senses to visit now and again, whether I like it or not. It doesn't happen often, but when it comes, my senses derange and everything transforms in an instant: I am young again, and happy, and the world is all alive around me. Last week I walked past a pool in the gymnasium of the university where I teach. The sting of chlorine in my nose pulled me forward and before I knew it I had fallen into a memory of fertile earth, marigolds, and the syrupy wash of plum on my tongue. My exquisite, tenacious ghosts collected around me, and there it was: the sweet, salty stickiness of skin; the sound of Denis' voice saying my name; the pang of knowing I never thanked him.

And then I shook my head and looked around; I was safe again, and alone, and I walked on to wherever it was I was supposed to go.

H.O.M.E.S.

Fernanda called to him from across the street, "Hey stupido, you make me sick," and all he could think to say back was "Shut up," but really loud. A moment later he added "Ugly," just before she opened the screen door and went into her house. Fernanda Hector-Caballo was in Mrs. Lutz's fourth grade class with Gerard. The walk home from school was a straight line down Hazelton Street for seven blocks to his house, and Fernanda lived smack in the center of that straight line at the bottom of a short hill. Her green slate house was on the corner of Hazelton and Euclid, its red front door facing Euclid, so that even though she passed the side door to her house first, she always walked the extra few feet to circle around to the front door, just in case, it seemed to him, she had one more thing to say.

Gerard couldn't remember exactly how or why, but sometime between second grade and fourth grade, he and Fernanda had begun walking home together on opposite sides of the street, and as they walked, they would yell mean things across to each other.

It may have started on the playground. There were seven of them playing four-square. Gerard, Fernanda, and Melanie were taking their turns outside of the square making fun of Riley Berger, who smelled. Fernanda told Melanie: "Stay away from that Riley boy. Mi Mami say if you smell a boy's underpits you might fall in love with him."

When Gerard heard that, he lifted his mouth to the blue-white sky and let out a whoop of laughter. Then he came up from behind Fernanda, wrangled her into a head-lock with her face in his underarm, and would not let go until she bit him.

The summer before his sister, Rachel, lost her hair to the chemotherapy, Gerard and Rachel would walk in the warm evenings to the Dairy Queen across from the school. The Hector-Caballos had a large wooden fence painted red, which blocked anyone from the street from seeing into the corner lot of their back yard. Behind the fence, Rachel and Gerard often heard someone playing a guitar, and there was a woman singing in a language their mother told them was Spanish. The thin breeze smelled of grasshoppers and of the river, which was only a few blocks away. Rachel's skips and wriggles grew more fervent the closer they got to the music, which hung low on the early evening air. On the way home, when the colors of the sky grew deeper, they'd slow down to listen, and sometimes stop, hushed across the street, licking the ice cream as it dripped down over their fingers.

One night, on the way to the Dairy Queen, the woman was singing as usual, and Rachel demanded Gerard's attention.

"Watch me, Gerard. Look. Watch this," she said as she twitched her hips three times in a row, turned on one heel, and began to spin quickly around and around and around, flailing her arms and stomping her feet, almost in time with the music.

"Stop acting like a goof-ball and come on," Gerard said. When she stopped, she almost fell. The rest of the way there, Rachel listed to one side, giggling as she exaggerated her dizziness. On the way home, they were both surprised. Behind the red wood fence at the Hector-Caballo's, a man with a deep voice sang a slow sad song. Gerard tried to concentrate on the words, hoping he could make the Spanish words turn into English just by paying closer attention. Then the man's voice shifted into a deep moan that rose and ended with the sound "Aaaiiiieeeee," and Gerard felt as though anything was possible; his heart could lift out of his body and flutter into the purple summer evening sky.

Rachel had spent most of second grade at home. Miss Waters, who tutored Rachel three evenings a week, wore scarves and smelled like spring, and every time she stepped from Rachel's room into the living room to say hello to Gerard he felt like it was his birthday. When she stayed for dinner, Gerard told her his favorite subject was Geography, and the next time she came over, she gave him a pack of fifty cards with a blue map of the United States on the front of each card with one of the states in red. On the back of each card were the state name and its capital city with pictures of the state bird and the state flower.

"Here's Michigan," Miss Waters told Gerard. She pointed to the card with her knuckle. "And here you are, right here: Detroit," she said.

It didn't seem like school. She would ask him questions, but he never felt stupid when he didn't know the answer. How lucky Rachel was, he thought. Another time Miss Waters brought him a map that showed all the bodies of water in North America. She had been in Rachel's room for an extra long time that night, and when she came out, Miss Waters and his mother talked in whispers in the kitchen. Gerard had come in to get a glass of milk, hoping he could hear them, but his mother stopped abruptly when she saw him, and told Gerard to go play in the den while she and Miss Waters talked.

"I'll come to say good-bye before I leave, Gerard. I've got something for you," Miss Waters had said.

Finally, his mother came to get him. "Come say good-bye to Miss Waters, Honey." She walked slowly ahead of Gerard with both her arms folded across her chest. Miss Waters sat on the sofa in the living room.

"I've got another map for you, Gerard. Do you remember what Michigan looks like on a map?" she asked before laying it down. Gerard held up his left hand, looked at it on the knuckles side, then turned his hand to show Miss Waters.

"That's right," she said. She unfolded the map and held it to her chest, cradling it like a prize. "Do you know why it looks like a mitten?"

"The peninsulas?"

"Well, yes. That's very good Gerard. Your teachers must love having you in their classes." Gerard stood leaning one hip against the arm of the sofa as his mother brought Miss Waters her coat. "What gives the peninsulas their shape, do you think?"

"Oh yeah," he said. "The Great Lakes."

"And what are their names?"

He could only remember Lake Michigan and Lake Erie.

"An easy way to remember," she said, " is if you take the first letter of each lake, and then put them together." She spread the map out on the floor of the living room and sat down with her knees together and her legs tucked off to one side. She patted the floor next to her, and Gerard sat down too. "They spell a word: H.O.M.E.S. Huron, Ontario, Michigan, Erie, and Superior."

Gerard felt powerful knowing something other kids didn't. He realized that if he told someone, then they'd know it too, and they'd be just as powerful as he was, so he decided to keep it to himself for a while. He'd carry it around with him, like a spy.

Every once in a while, Fernanda would not come to school and Gerard would wonder why. Did she cry and ask her mother to please let her stay home? Was she really sick, or faking sick? Was she at home right now secretly touching the strings of her father's guitar?

He felt sorry for her some days when she'd miss the best things, like Michael Healey throwing up in the coat room, or Mary Jane Urquhart bringing in the bone she'd found in her back yard, or the time she missed the announcements about their parts in the school's

Halloween play. He wanted to go to Fernanda and tell her everything she'd missed. He wanted her to ask him.

When she came back to school after a day or two gone she looked just the same; she was neither thin nor pale nor sad, nor even rested. Only sometimes, when they walked home on those days after she'd been gone, she seemed to hate him more than ever. And he wondered if, when she was home from school, she ever thought about him and about how much she loved to scream at him from across the way.

Rachel's sickness started with a ball he had thrown. They were playing catch in the backyard when the ball hit Rachel's knee. She was fine at the time, but then she screamed in pain the whole rest of the night. His mother had asked him: "Why can't you ever play nice?" and his father had asked: "Do you see what can happen when you act like a fool?"

But when the doctors told them it was leukemia, they said it was a good thing Gerard had hit her with the ball when he did. Catching the leukemia early greatly improved her prognosis, they'd said. Had it gone much longer she'd only have a fifty-fifty chance instead of a seventy-five percent chance of survival; and when his parents heard this, they almost thanked Gerard for having thrown the ball at her, even though he'd told them he didn't mean to do it. It really was an accident.

It was so strange. One week Gerard and Rachel were writing their names in their new school notebooks, walking to school together, swimming and running through the sprinkler in the last of the summer heat. The next week his whole house became sad and stayed that way.

On the Wednesday during her second course of chemo, Rachel began to cry at the dinner table.

"What's wrong Rachel?" her father asked.

"I'm not hungry," she said very slowly, and by the time she got to the word "hungry," her voice had risen to a wail.

Gerard watched the confusion in his parents' faces, because this was something he had never seen. The wailing kept up, everyone else silent and staring at Rachel, thinking that at some point she had to stop, but she didn't.

"Shut up!" Gerard finally yelled at her, but as soon as he did, his mother screamed, "Gerard, YOU shut up!" She got up and pushed some of the food around on Rachel's plate, as if rearranging it could make her eat. "Rachel, just eat what you can, dear," she said.

Rachel pushed her seat back from the table, stood on top of it, picked up her plate and threw it against the wall.

"It's the prednisone," his mother explained to him later. "The same pills that make her swell up and get puffy also make her really mean sometimes. She's going to have to take them for the last week of every month for a long time, so we just have to expect it, and be especially patient with her."

"How long?" Gerard had wanted to know. The chemo had started just after he'd entered fourth grade.

"A long time. A few years. The doctors say two and a half to three years. You'll be in seventh grade by then."

Gerard tried to imagine time, but it was all white with tiny spots like the television during a storm when the wind knocks over the antenna. The only thing he could think of was all the homework he'd have to do between now and seventh grade.

"I know it's hard for you, honey. It's hard for all of us, especially Rachel."

By Halloween, Rachel's hair was gone, and she had swollen up like she was stuffed with cotton. He couldn't believe how ugly she had become. Sometimes in the morning he'd come out of the bathroom and catch a glimpse of her, having forgotten that she had changed. It felt like the bottom of his stomach was gone.

Gerard noticed that his mother had found a new way of talking that included words and parts of words that made it seem like a foreign language, but he knew it wasn't Spanish. When she talked this way, the bones around his father's eyes pushed forward with concentration, making them look much smaller than they were, and the vein above his right temple came out. The only other time Gerard had seen this look was at times like when Rachel had thrown her doll at Gerard, but missed and instead hit her father in the head. "Rachel," his father had said between his teeth, the bump on his head almost as big as the blue-white vein that throbbed near his eye, "that really hurt, Honey. You know you shouldn't throw things at people."

One night at dinner, after his mother had had what she called "a bad Rachel day," she began to describe a new symptom she thought Rachel might be developing.

His father got that look and said only, "Please," and left the table with all the food still on his plate.

After that night his mother turned to Gerard. "Infection," she would say. "Hemorrhage. But these are only possibilities. Don't be too alarmed, because they may not happen." Secretly, just in case one day his mother asked, Gerard learned to spell these words by looking in her new medical dictionary, which she kept on the coffee table. "Ataxia. That's from the vincristine. It describes her funny walk, the way her feet slap the ground, but they say it will go away when the chemo is done."

Sometimes he would listen and learn, but other times he would answer her: "Did you know the Mississippi River flows north to south and is 2348 miles long?" She would look at him with a face stern and blank as a starched uniform, smooth both hands over both knees, and leave him alone with his books and maps.

Gerard's father came to the Halloween play while his mother stayed home with Rachel. They were doing Charlie Brown's Great Pumpkin, with dance skits inserted using old pop songs.

Gerard was one of the regular pumpkins. Fernanda was the lead dancing pumpkin who danced to the song "Time after Time" behind Linus while he waits for the Great Pumpkin, who never shows up. From the back of the stage, Gerard watched Fernanda mix graceful bends with awkward steps. He heard someone in the audience giggle and another person laugh, and he thought, "I'd like to see them try to do that." Fernanda's dance looked like she meant to do it that way. It seemed to Gerard exactly right.

When it was over, and the pounding of dancing pumpkin feet had stopped resounding over the stage, Fernanda's mouth grew tight and red, and she ran off the stage crying. Gerard didn't know if it was because she was happy, or sad, or embarrassed. Mrs. Lutz went to get her and brought her back on the stage, and Fernanda stood obediently on the slippery, shiny wood while her father stood in the audience whooping and clapping, moving his head from side to side, and then around behind him, looking at everyone to make sure they knew this was his daughter, as Fernanda's mother tugged on his shirt sleeve from where she sat next to him.

When Gerard sat in the living room's green armchair with the raised paisley swirls in the fabric, he could hear every word his mother said when she was on the phone in the kitchen. He learned a lot this way. Lately he had learned how much his mother missed night school, and even missed working at the shoe store. Last year he had learned how his parents first met at the shoe store, his father having bought three pair of shoes there before he found the courage to ask her out. He learned how his Uncle Charlie's wife was a bitch who they were nice to only for Charlie's sake.

Recently he had learned that his mother didn't regret taking the time off from her life to take care of Rachel, and at this he imagined his mother standing with a time card outside of a big factory that was her life, with Gerard and his father inside looking out at her and Rachel.

One night Gerard heard his mother tell someone: "I don't know what I'd do if we lost her." He hadn't thought about that, and he became frightened. He had heard stories of lost children. There were kids being kidnapped, strangers preying on small children, luring them into cars with candy and then snatching them up and driving away. They had even shown a video in Mrs. Lutz's class. "Don't talk to strangers," it said. "Walk straight home after school. Don't linger." What was happening with Rachel seemed no different. He missed the old Rachel, the one who let him draw pictures so she could color them, the one who held his hand when they walked across the street together, the one with long straight hair that hung down to the middle of her back when she walked, but which, when he pushed her on the swing, spun up and out as beautiful as the spider webs he'd seen in the mornings on the bushes. There were still times when they sat together on the sofa, him singing and stroking her arm while she asked questions, but other times she was a mean, ugly puffy monster who screamed and ran around the house, and then sometimes disappeared for three days in a row. If it could happen to her, it could happen to anyone. No one was safe.

Fernanda hadn't been in school for two days. When Mrs. Lutz came to her name during roll call, she said Fernanda's name more as a whisper to herself than as a question to which she expected an answer the way she said everyone else's name. It was the week before Thanksgiving.

That day he walked home on Fernanda's side of the street, just to see what it was like. He liked his side better because there were more trees. On his side, the branches jutted out like friendly arms waving hello to him as he walked past. Fernanda's side had mostly bushes up against the houses, and the people on her side of the street didn't seem to take care of their front lawns as well. One house even had a car parked right on the front lawn.

As he approached the corner where Fernanda's house sat, he noticed that between the garage and the red wood fence was a short span of wire cyclone fence, where he could look into the back yard, and even see the back of her house. Rows of tall bushes separated the fence between the Hector-Caballo's yard from their next-door neighbor's. He made sure no one was watching before he threw his backpack over the fence and climbed in.

The grass in their yard was long, reaching past Gerard's ankles. He wandered around waiting for something to happen, but nothing did.

The windows at the back of her house were too high for him to see into the house on his own. He had to lift up the wooden picnic table alternately one end at a time, and scuttle his slippery shoes through the tall grass in order to get it underneath one of the two windows.

The evening light had not faded completely. With hands cupped around both sides of his head, he peered into the window through the slits in the curtain, hoping to see a guitar, castanets, or a red dress with fringe, but all he could make out was the rough fabric of the beige curtain and a bulge that looked like the arm of an old chair.

He sat down on the picnic table and looked around. He could do anything he wanted here. There would be no way he could get into trouble, unless he broke something. He thought about that for a minute, looking around for something in Fernanda's yard to break. There was a tiny white fence about six inches high that went around the garage. There were dead plants, and small rocks.

The dirt in the little garden was hard and broke into clumps that Gerard picked up and threw at the white paint of the garage, leaving little black marks. He picked up a clump and tried to think of something to write in dirt on the garage. The only word he could think of was guitar, but didn't know how to spell that, so instead he began with "Fernanda is." He couldn't think of a good word to finish with, so he threw down the dirt and instead ran and slid through the grass for a home run.

It was getting late, and it was getting dark, and when the cars drove down the street, their headlights flashed through the cyclone fence and threw weird shadows on the grass. Gerard pretended they were intruders and fought them off, karate-chopping them back into invisibility.

A car slowed down and stopped by the short driveway in front of the Hector-Caballo's garage. There was no easy way out, since the fence was right next to the garage door; surely they'd see him if he tried to escape. Gerard crouched behind the garage and stretched his neck around the corner of it to see what was happening. The car wasn't moving, and he didn't hear the door open or close. If he got caught, he could say he was just trying to bring Fernanda her homework. If he had to, he could climb through the bushes over the fence into the neighbor's yard. He put his backpack on, leaned against the garage, ready for anything. He imagined climbing over fence after fence, the car tracking him from the street with a flashlight shining into all their neighbors' back yards, Fernanda hanging out of the car window yelling things at him as he fled for the park at the end of the block, and then to the river.

Soon enough he heard a car door open and shut. A woman's voice, clear and American, said, "Thanks again, Bill. Good night, and have a happy Thanksgiving." Then the car drove off. He heard her heels click across to the other side of the street, the yawn of the screen door opening, then the slam of the front door shutting the cold night out of her home.

After that, he pretended every car that came down the street was the Hector-Caballo's so that he could dive to safety and roll through the grass out of view.

It had become dark. The fenced-in back yard made the evening seem like the middle of the night. Gerard knew his parents would wonder where he was, and he was glad and tired. When he climbed back over the fence and onto the sidewalk, there was no one on the street and no cars were coming, so he knew he had escaped without anyone knowing he was there.

When he got home, his mother was crying. She ran up to him and squeezed him hard.

"Sweetie, are you okay? I'm so sorry. I'm so sorry."

He told her "Mom, it's okay."

"Listen," she said, "If that ever happens again, you go right over to Mrs. Lester's house. And if she's not home, we'll give you a key so you can get in." Gerard shook himself away to take off his backpack.

"You must have been so frightened," she said. "We had to take Rachel to the hospital. She spiked a temp." It sounded like a sports term to him, something he could say to one of his classmates about some sort of ball. He kicked off both shoes and left them in the middle of the living room floor. His father clinked pots and pans in the kitchen, opened cupboards to get ready for dinner.

"Where did you go, anyway?" she added. "What did you do?"

"Nowhere," he said. "Nothing."

His mother picked his backpack up off the floor and held it on her knees.

There were no lights on in the living room, so when his father stood in the doorway that led to the kitchen, the light from behind stretched his shadow across Gerard's mother's body. "We're out of milk," he said.

"The doctors say she'll only have to stay a few days," his mother continued to Gerard. "You can go visit her tomorrow. She misses you. She'll want to see you."

From the kitchen doorway Gerard heard, "Gerard, why don't you come with me to the store?" He slumped down hard on the couch with both arms crossed over his chest in response. "I'll get the car," his father said. "Meet me out front."

Gerard sat silently on the couch. When his mother moved to brush the hair out of his eyes, he jerked away, put his shoes and coat on, and tromped out to the porch to wait for his father to pull the car up.

The short buildings they passed on the way to the store were mostly gray or brown brick, or white aluminum siding. The ones that weren't gas stations or fast food restaurants had black letters announcing their names: Steelco Tool and Die, or Bob's Auto Parts, or Motor City Heating and Cooling.

On the way home from the supermarket, his father said, "Do you want to see where Miss Waters teaches during the day?"

Gerard answered, "I don't care," but was glad when his father turned a corner Gerard knew was not the way home. The school was in Dearborn, and it was huge. Gerard's school had eight classrooms -- one room for each grade. Miss Waters' school towered three stories high, and Gerard wondered what it would be like to have kids in your same grade who you never even met.

Driving home on the expressway, his father pointed to the Uniroyal tire, a giant black tire that loomed over I-94, even taller than Miss Waters' school. "The first time I saw that," his father said, "all I could think of was what kind of car would have a tire that big, and what would it be like to drive it. It could run over anything that got in your way."

"Yeah," Gerard said, and he meant it.

Gerard had been to the Pediatric Ward twice before to visit Rachel. Most of the time Rachel slept, Gerard grew bored, and his parents let him wander in the halls and in the playroom where he met other kids. The first time, he'd met a kid his own age who had gotten into a car accident with his mother and father. The kid had a broken arm and leg, and both his parents had been killed. He told Gerard he could go with the casts on when the hospital found him a new home. The hospital people told him he'd probably go live with his grandparents, but they were on vacation or something, and the hospital didn't know how to contact them yet.

Then there was the last time, with the room at the end of Rachel's hall where nurses marched in and out more than any other room on the floor. When Gerard walked past, he heard all kinds of beeps and gurgles. He never heard any voices or crying. There were no signs on the door saying he had to put on a mask or gown the way there was on Rachel's door. The door stayed open with the yellow curtain always drawn.

The same room was there this time too, with the same beeps and gurgles.

Gerard decided to explore.

No one had gone into that room for a long time. He walked down the hall secret-agent style, affecting the intent nonchalance of a man on a mission. He pretended to look at the pictures of balloons, and horses, and flowers that hung on the walls, and when he got to the room with the curtain, he snuck in. He stood just inside the door and faced the yellow curtain, trying to make out if there was a nurse or a parent or someone moving behind it. The room smelled old, like a mixture of a bathroom and a dentist's office. The beeps and buzzes grew louder. He slipped quickly past the curtain to look in the bed, and there he saw a monster. It had a body like a child, but the arms and legs were scrunched up; its fingers and toes curled under in what looked like a permanent cramp. The head, bigger than the rest of the body, was watermelon-shaped, with the skin stretched pink and white so tightly over the face that it looked like it would soon burst. Worst of all, one of the eyes bulged out, all white except for a little dot of black on the end of the white, cone shaped pupil. Suddenly the smell became stronger and worse than anything else he had ever smelled. When he moved a little to the left, the eye twitched to follow him. Unable to breath or to scream, he ran out of the room, and fell down on the floor in the hall.

A nurse found him with his hands over his head, face down on the floor.

"Who are you?" she said when she sat him up. "Where are you supposed to be?" But he couldn't answer. The horrible smell of the room, and the sight of the water-melon head with the eye filled up his whole head and pushed everything else out of it, until he felt maybe he was becoming the monster kid, or that that's how Rachel might end up. He sat on the floor staring at the nurse. She was saying something like, "It's okay. It's okay. Everything is going to be okay." He kept staring at the nurse, looking at the expressions on her normal face, watching her mouth make words, and wondering what they meant.

"Hydrocephalic," his mother tried to explain to him later, "water on the brain." No matter how hard he tried, Gerard couldn't understand, and he wasn't sure he wanted to know any more.

Rachel came home in less than a week. When he went back to school, he learned Fernanda had gone to Colombia, South America with her parents to visit their family during Thanksgiving break. Mrs. Lutz pulled the string from a long aluminum tube that hung in the front of the classroom to show them a map of the world.

"Where is Colombia, Fernanda?" Mrs. Lutz asked. Fernanda walked to the front of the class and pointed to Colombia with the wooden pointer Mrs. Lutz had placed in her hand. She showed them the city of Cali, where she had been born, and then pointed to Detroit, to show how far apart they were in the world. Out of the bag she had brought in that day, Fernanda took a blanket that had all sorts of designs in red and blue and yellow and orange. She said her grandmother had made it for her, and explained how everything in Colombia was more colorful than in Detroit.

"We can understand a lot about the world by knowing where we live, and by appreciating where other people live," Mrs. Lutz told them.

That night, Gerard went home to find Rachel in her room coloring with his colored pencils. She had lost a little of her puffiness, and hair sprouted on her head in fine tufts. He helped her trace the fingers of her hand on paper so she could draw a turkey like the one he had brought home the week before. Her thumb became the head of the turkey, and the rest of her fingers became the feathers of the tail. While she colored in the turkey's tail, he closed his fingers and traced his hand again on another sheet of paper, to make the shape of Michigan. He traced the figure of his left hand on the paper, then drew in the edges of Wisconsin, Illinois, Indiana, Ohio, the Upper Peninsula, and Canada. With the blue pencil he colored the lakes, and then in black wrote in their names with the first letter of each lake bigger than the rest so that he could teach Rachel the trick of how to remember them. On the bottom right of the map he drew stick figures; one with glasses for his dad, one with a dress for his mom, a smaller figure for himself, and another small figure with long hair curling down to its feet as Rachel. Underneath the picture he wrote the word "Detroit" and put a big red dot there.

Rachel was still working on her picture on the floor, so Gerard went and brought in a book on birds he had in his room. He sat on the bed and read to her while she drew. He read about how hummingbirds beat their wings up to ninety times a second, and that some common swifts can stay in the air for three years at a time without landing. He wondered what it would be like to fly around for three years, up in the air the whole time, never having to worry about going to school or coming home. Rachel began to whimper because her hand was getting tired, but when she came over to sit by him on the bed, she didn't say a word. She just looked at the pictures in his book as he flipped the pages. Before he knew it she was asleep again, her head on his lap, and he made sure not to move an inch, or touch her in any way.

PROOF

The porch light is on at 4 pm when it isn't even dusk yet, so the bushes on the right side of our yard look taller than usual, the awning appears slanted to the left, and the lawn throws off a beige tinge when I pull into the driveway to square the car off against the door of the garage. For a few minutes I sit collecting notebooks filled with quizzes I need to grade. A paper from one of my better students sits on top of the stack with the answer to the first problem written in pencil so dark it looks like it's engraved. I run my fingertips over the dark marks scratched onto what was once clean white paper, but today even Lan Nguyen's delicate triangles and octagons from fourth period Geometry fail to set the world back on kilter.

Neither Anne nor our son Sammy are home, but Anne has scrawled a note on the 4x4 pad of multicolored sticky notes I brought home from work to leave by the phone in the kitchen. This one is light blue and stuck to the kitchen table: Abe -- Sammy in trouble at school. Back soon. Make dinner.

There is only a little hamburger in the freezer, and I'm not in the mood for chicken pot pies. Just as I finish ordering the pizza, Anne's car pulls into the driveway.

Anne looks straight ahead as she parks. Sammy barely waits for the car to stop moving before he gets out. I say "Hey" to Sammy when he walks in the front door, but he won't look at me. His mouth, which is round and full, looks unnatural like this, stuck in a straight line.

"Hey," Anne says. "I have to go to the bathroom. I'll be back in a minute."

Sammy goes directly to the refrigerator. When I tell him I've just ordered pizza, he slams the door closed and says, "Just looking," in a tone I've never heard him use before; it's angry and impatient in a way that is familiar only because I'd sometimes heard it in my replies to my own parents when I was slightly older than Sammy is now.

Anne comes back into the room and says, "Did he tell you?"

I chuckle, "No, no one tells me anything." When she doesn't even smile I say, "What?"

"I got in trouble," Sammy says to fill the silence Anne has laid out for him. He sits at the kitchen table and won't look at anything other than the fraying white thread of a hole in his blue jeans, which he combs back and forth the whole time we talk.

"He killed the class hamster."

"On purpose?" I say.

"He sealed the hamster in a plastic lunch bag." This doesn't answer my question so I look to Sammy for clarification.

Sammy moves the salt and pepper shakers to the exact center of the table, shrugs his shoulders and lets the line of his mouth relax. The blood comes back into his lips, making them round and full again, redder than ever.

Alberto Zapata teaches Spanish in room 302, I'm Math in 304, and Julie Washington is English in 303.

Every year Alberto walks into his room and writes a huge Z on the board with the muscular swish of Zorro and turns dramatically to say "Zapata. Señor Zapata to you." He's a pretty happy guy. As far as teaching in Detroit goes, we're all pretty happy here at Renaissance High. It's a magnet school for honors students, so we get the highest caliber students. Because he's both handsome and charming, the kids work harder to please Alberto, even the boys. It's just a fact. Ugly teachers have to work a lot harder. If you're really ugly, you can still be effective as long as you're funny. It's the dumpy teachers, the bland ones who have nothing strange or real to offer, who are dead meat.

I'm goofy looking, but I'm funny, at least that's what my student evaluations say: Mr. Lansfeld is boring when he talks about Math, but otherwise he's funny. Or, It's harder to fall asleep in Lansfeld's class. He cracks me up.

Julie is small featured and thin, tall and lanky and full of caffeine. She always wears big shoes and some version of a black sweater to highlight her tawny brown complexion: cashmere, cotton, or tight knit polyester with an orange racing stripe, for instance. One of her hips is always jutting out in one direction or another. She's pretty, but not the least bit graceful. All her entrances include the feel of an explosion or the placement of a bomb. She plops rather than sits, trips and drops more than walks or carries, lands and settles instead of leaning or resting on something. And if all this were the least bit of an affectation, I would hate her, but it's not, so I think she's great, and so does anyone with even a little bit of sense.

The teachers' lounge has the same blue and orange plastic chairs that are in the student cafeteria. Alberto says the faded blue and orange swirls in the formica table tops look like little sperm.

I tell them about Sammy and the hamster and ask them what they think.

"I had a friend who used to kill cats and dogs for a living when we were young," Alberto tells me. "In our village, strays crept through every street. The butcher and the baker? They said, 'No way!' Together they hired Paulo. Paulo was so fast; he'd grab them quick, strangle them, drown them, bludgeon them, whatever, then bring them to the butcher. They gave him sometimes money, sometimes breads and cakes for every corpse he brought in. The butcher kept an enormous furnace at the back of his shop to burn the parts of pigs and cows nobody would buy. He threw the carcasses in there. At least we all hoped he did."

"Alberto," Julie says, "you're the only person I know who can make peanut butter and jelly seem gruesome and unappetizing." She throws her sandwich onto the wax paper with a thunk. After a moment she picks it up again and bites out a gigantic hunk, smearing jelly on both cheeks, smiling a broad peanut butter speckled smile.

"The point, my friend," and he cups his hand around the back of my neck and rubs in small circles, "is don't worry. Is no big deal."

"What happened to Paulo?" I ask.

Alberto becomes confused and says, "Well, I'm not sure, exactly." He remains silent for an uncomfortably long time. "He probably joined the Peace Corps so he could work in a sewer in some well-developed nation."

"No, what really happened to him," says Julie.

"Really? I don't know. He disappeared one day and we never heard from him again."

There is a spasm between my eyebrows.

"But probably he saved enough money to get out of that hell-hole. He was a local hero. An inspiration to me. That's why I left."

Alberto wraps his arm around my neck and squeezes, pulling me into his chest so close I can smell the clean warm scent of his underarm deodorant.

It's 3:30 pm, so I have two more hours before I pick up Sammy from his piano lesson at Beth McCall's house. Anne has typed a note and printed it out to leave on the kitchen table. She does this every once in a while, and it disturbs me probably more than it should. If she'd just text me, she could tell me what she wants immediately instead of wasting time and paper. She's gone back to law school and still works every other weekend as a pharmacist at the hospital. I know she's unbelievably busy, but I think if someone is going to communicate with me mostly through paper notes, I at least want the impression that there was a pulse or a touch of body heat on the page at one point in its history. The note says in its clipped type face: *abe you need to call the principal again something about sammy.*

I take the note and walk up the musty stairs into my study, which is really a walk-in closet in the attic that has a nice little space for a desk just under a window. A pile of Anne's notes lie under a snow globe that shows Dorothy and Toto and company sleeping in the poppy field. Every once in a while I shake it to make it snow. "Wake up," I say, "Wake up. You have to get to Oz. You need a brain, a heart, the noyve." I used to shake it for Sammy when he was little and say, "There's no place like home. There's no place like home." Today I pick it up and put it on top of some books while I leaf through Anne's old notes to me.

The window looks out over the front yard, and I can see a long way down the street into the front yards of our neighbors. This is a great time of year. October, the leaves of maple and oak trees are still laced with a green that's beginning to fade, letting the other colors bleed through: the reds, oranges, yellows, colors that are there all the time, but stay hidden until chlorophyll production stops in the leaves and they no longer produce the green.

Looking down at the street like this I could almost stop breathing. There's no way to control all this beauty. It's right there in front of you whether you're ready for it or not. And if you're not, then it moves along without you. Who can ever pay close enough attention?

Sammy's been taking piano lessons since he was six years old. I'm sorry to admit our decision had as much to do with our own free time as it did with his development as a person. Maybe more. Something that sounds vaguely close to Mozart shakes the wooden floor boards of Beth McCall's porch. I stand there for a minute or so before I ring the bell to see if I can tell anything about my son that I should know, but don't, by listening to the sounds he's making with the piano keys. When I'm satisfied that no, I still don't know anything, I ring the bell. Beth's head of thick, kinky red hair surprises me every time I see it, even though I've known her most of my life. Her house has that curious smell of dust and raisins common to these old Rosedale Park houses.

Sammy's still at the piano bench arranging the contents of his back pack when I get to the piano room.

"Hi Dad," he says without looking up.

I wait for him to look at me before I say hello, but he won't do it. About five seconds later, though it feels much longer, I slide next to him on the smooth cherry wood bench and say, "How'd it go today?" I put my hand on the back of his head and play with the soft hair there. He doesn't pull away. My ribs shake like the floor boards of the porch in gratitude.

Instead of an answer, he grunts as he bends down to get his baseball cap to replace my hand. Beth comes in and talks to him about which lessons he should learn for next week, and asks him if he thinks he's ready for Schubert. Sammy's answers are perfunctory, and as I watch him I think of what kind of a punk my little boy could become.

There's a boy named Kirk Stout, a sophomore, in fourth period Geometry. If he weren't smart he wouldn't have gotten in to Renassaince High, but there's something else wrong. At the beginning of the year they handed me a file on him that took up three folders describing family social history and school related problems. I know he attacked a teacher once, picked up a podium and threw it at the guy. Kirk can get straight A's when he wants to, or he can fail if he decides he's bored with something, anything. He got the highest score on the first exam I gave, but then there was a month when he came in almost every day and buried his head in the crook of his elbow and slept through class. For the past week he's been yessirring me and acting real attentive, which makes me more nervous. I have no idea how he will turn out, if anything I say makes any difference at all to him, but this is true for almost anyone we come in contact with, isn't it? It's just nicer to feel you can take credit for the good ones. People never discuss their possible influence on evil-doers, the mistakes that may have spawned a despicable situation.

I don't want my son to be anything like Kirk Stout. Kirk Stout is miserable.

I've drifted away completely, and Beth looks at me. She's biting the inside of her cheek, her mouth pursed to the side. Sammy's leaning against the door waiting for me. This used to be the point when he'd lean into me. Somewhere between ten and eleven someone decided it wasn't cool to hug your father, that a boy of eleven should spurn any connection but an anonymous nod to parents. Sometimes I still think he wants to hug me, but holds himself back. The restraint embarrasses us both.

Just last year, if I put my hand on his shoulder he'd bury his face in my coat and inhale deeply. I used to do the same thing with my father. The mixture of the smell of burning leaves and my father's after shave and pipe made me feel that very little could ever go wrong. I haven't thought of that smell in years, and I suddenly miss my father very much, miss my wife, miss the whole fucking world, and hate it too. I stand in a neighbor's house looking at my son only an arm's length away, wanting everything that's not possible, understanding I will never be enough for him.

Anne said she'd be at the library until about nine o'clock. Sammy and I eat Chinese take-out and play checkers, which we've done before, but tonight I wonder if it feels fake to him too, if he knows I'm trying to keep him away from the T.V. It's strange to suddenly begin monitoring everything he watches on television, but I don't care. We live in Detroit, where a distance of only a few blocks can tell a tale of homey comfort or total desperation. There's so much he might have already seen.

We've tried to entertain him with old movies, classics. Once, he shouted out "seven minutes" while a movie was playing; he'd been timing the length of the scenes the director filmed before taking a cut. That's brilliant. I think that's brilliant. How could a kid like that be bad?

But right now he's trying to lose quickly at checkers to get the game over with, and I'm refusing to bite. I can play as poorly as the next guy, and if he wants to lose, he's going to have to fight for it. There's barely enough room at the board to move through the patchwork of red and black since neither of us will take any more of the other's checkers.

Sammy leans back and says, "Dad, I don't want to play anymore."

"Why not?" I ask.

"It's boring."

All my cheery good humor is gone. In school I can crank into charm overdrive -- which sometimes works and sometimes doesn't -- but Sammy knows me too well.

"Sam," I say, "What's the problem here?"

"Nothing," he says, and though he slumps back into his chair taking the posture of a limp doll with half the stuffing gone, I know this is his way of squirming.

"I wanted to wait until your Mom came home, but we need to talk about what happened."

"What?" he says.

"The hamster."

"It's dead," he says.

"I know." This conversation feels as doomed as our checker game, but I can't find any way to change its course. I refuse to let it go.

"Someone dared me to do it, so I did."

"How do you feel about it?"

"Feel?" he says, and I know this is what I've been dreading all along: the question mark after the word "feel" that slices the air between us.

When he begins to cry I'm not sure if it's because he's sad about what he did, or sad about getting into trouble for it, or just putting on a show for me. But for now, it's enough. We watch a special called "Storm Chasers" on the nature channel about people who hunt tornadoes to film them and the destruction they leave behind before Sammy heads up for bed early.

Anne comes home to a quiet house.

I put the note Anne left me on her pillow so that she'll have to talk to me about it. Lately she's been trying on new attitudes. She's learning how to brush away the small details of her life to look at a grander, more tragic picture: society as a whole -- a phrase I've always found wholly inadequate as a description of anything even close to something you can use to guide your day.

"Did you remember to turn off the porch light?" I ask.

"Mm," she says. "I think."

"You think?"

She picks the note up and folds it into fours, sets it on the night table next to our bed, and plops on the bed face down into the pillow.

"He's been begging his science teacher to dissect frogs," I say. "He told her he'd even catch one for her. Mrs. Dunne didn't think much about it until the hamster incident. 'Now we're forced to think of all the possible ramifications,' she said. That's the word she used, Anne: ramifications."

"Come on, Abe." Anne's muffled voice comes up from the pillow before she turns her head to train one gray eye on me. "He's not some freak. He's our son. He's as normal as any other kid."

"I know," I say, relieved someone is finally reassuring me. "I mean my god, what's wrong with these teachers? Ramifications of wanting to dissect a frog. It's only natural to want to know how things work." I'm beginning to convince myself everything will be okay.

Anne says, "Yeah, but isn't that how Jeffrey Dahmer got his start?" The comment startles Anne as much as it does me, because we know it's true, and we both laugh a little too hard.

No parents want to think of their child as a monstrosity, either born or created. It's possible that we've messed up somehow. It's like that Larkin poem that Julie recited to me and Alberto: "They fuck you up, your mum and dad." It's the one that ends by saying you should never have kids. After she recited it, we all had a good laugh. Neither one of them has a child.

I say to Anne, "What do a few separate instances prove?" But I know it takes only two points to make a line, and this scares me to death.

We end up talking about Sammy as if he's some sort of science experiment. He's normal. He keeps his room clean, in fact he's unusually tidy; any semblance of disarray in him is a put on. He does have occasional fits of rage, but don't all children? Nothing is innocent anymore. One time, just after Anne started law school, we took Sammy to the mall to buy new school clothes. He was nine, then. Sammy started laughing really hard, neither Anne nor I could figure out at what. I've seen other kids do that before so we didn't pay much attention until he began to jump up and down in full view of the people in the GAP. His laugh sounded fake and forced, like something conjured up as a weapon. At one point he lay down, kicking his arms and legs. Anne and I talked about it later, but brushed it off as a sugar high from too much ice cream. Now, every little thing, every little little could be some sort of land mine waiting to blow us apart.

I want someone to set things out, to add them all up and draw a line under them and say, "This is the answer: Everything will always be fine," even if there's no possible way to believe it. If it's our fault maybe we can still fix it. If it's not, then nothing we do will matter. How can I hope it's our fault?

I could talk to him about death. Instead of telling him it's natural, it's nothing to be afraid of, I should tell him the truth: Death is not okay, it's not entertainment, it's not Halloween. Death is horrible. You should be afraid. Nothing will save us from it. You should do whatever you can to stay away from death. Don't touch it with a ten foot pole. Or a sealed plastic lunch bag.

"Not counseling. Not yet, Anne," I tell her. "I think he'll be okay. Counseling feels like admitting something, pleading guilty when you don't even know the crime."

"Abe," she tells me, "the crime is murder." She reminds me of that other incident last year when Sammy and Cal Jacobs put the cat on top of Cal's grandfather's revolving turntable just to see the cat hang on for dear life. Then they pushed it off so they could watch it walk around the room like a drunk.

I remember when Anne used to be kind.

We can't even control the things we create. Especially the things we create. When did the boundary between normal human cruelty and sociopathology get so blurry?

When I was little, I burnt ants and grasshoppers with a magnifying glass, and I've seen television shows use this as a joke, so I know other kids did that too. I also used to catch grasshoppers and burn them with the plastic from the army men I had set on fire. I'd let the hot green plastic cover the grasshopper's body with a slow crackle that sounded like Rice Crispies when you pour milk over them.

Maybe Sammy is just a bad gene gone worse.

Soon, if not already, Sammy will feel the stinging chemistry of sexuality. Hormones, peer pressure, a yearning to escape the horrors and boredom of the world. I've seen it before. Melanie Coyne, a girl in my Algebra I class two years ago: happy girl who is smart, willing to please, grows very large breasts and tries to fit in. High school and the theory of the bad crowd. She started segregating herself, only hanging out with the white kids, who make up less than a quarter of the student body.

She died in the middle of her sophomore year from an overdose of Crystal Meth, something that sounds more like a bad country singer than a drug.

Alberto and Julie went with me to Melanie's funeral. Julie said Melanie was the only child of a single parent. I guess I expected the mother to be a skinny, haggard woman with frizzy blond hair and dark yellow nicotine stains on her fingers. I never expected a fuller, more sophisticated, even prettier version of her daughter with an Hermès scarf. I never would have guessed she'd look like someone I would want to date if I weren't married to Anne. Someone with whom I could walk through a museum, show off to by making my spicy pasta sauce, someone I would want to kiss between her eyebrows, for a start.

I didn't lose it until we were at the graveside and saw Melanie's mother cry, which is how it always happens with me. I've never been a good witness to grief. I stood stiff and dumb, blinking away the blur of tears. Alberto, with his arm across my back, his strong hand on my shoulder. Julie with her sweet perfume on the other side holding my hand in hers, soft and warm. Me in the middle feeling helpless and stupid, trying on the grief of a woman I don't even know.

At night, in bed, Anne curls up next to me and talks about torts. We scheduled a meeting with Mr. Marcoux, Sammy's teacher. She crosses her feet at the ankles and jiggles them back and forth. She's either concentrating on something she's trying to memorize or she's working herself up to tell me something she knows I don't want to hear. Like her constant refrain that she wants to get away from Detroit forever.

But I'm wrong again. She says we should meet in the school parking lot at 10:45 since the appointment is at 11:00. We should walk in together.

"That's fine," I say.

"Good," Anne says. I feel like we're planning some covert operation. Then she surprises me by kissing me long and slow. She roots under my tee shirt and rubs her hand over my bare chest and stomach until I feel myself getting hard. I turn to hold her, reach under her pajama top and brush her nipple with my thumb. She pats my stomach three times with her hand and says, "Good night," reaches over me to turn off the light, then turns away, hugging her pillow instead of me.

We meet with Mr. Marcoux in Sammy's fifth grade classroom. He's short, but built like an athlete. He grips my hand firmly, almost aggressively. His black hair is flecked with gray, shaved on the sides with the braids on top falling attractively to the side over his ear. He's semi-famous because his brother is the meteorologist on channel four news, and I think for a moment Sammy's teacher could have been an actor rather than a teacher. The back wall has perfect spelling papers with big yellow stars at the top of each one next to the student's name. The other wall is taken up with windows and brown painted heating vents. On one shelf above the vents by the back windows sits the empty hamster cage. The smell of cedar overpowers the room.

Until now, I hadn't thought about the different ways a hamster might die. Right after we sit down, Mr. Marcoux begins the story with his lilting Haitian accent.

It was Sammy's turn to clean the hamster cage. Sammy had put Chico the hamster into the large plastic baggie that he'd kept from lunch and began shaking it.

"Look," someone heard him say, "shake and bake Chico." Ted Wight, whose mother donated the hamster, began to scream. He called Sammy a "fucking jerk," Mr. Marcoux says, emphasizing these words with two fingers of each hand stroking out quotation marks to show us his own sense of propriety. That's when Sammy thwacked the baggie hard on the heating vent and threw it across the room. The hamster baggie missed Ted Wight's head and hit the blackboard. Chico's skull cracked. One eye fell out and it bled a little, but the whole mess was self-contained in the baggie.

What is there to say? Anne begins to talk, to speak, to hold forth. My god, I've never seen her talk like this. She's proving to Mr. Marcoux that we are good parents, good people, a good family. We are good. Goodness is us.

I hear the words, "right," "wrong," and "justice," and I begin thinking about my own classroom. I dedicated room 304 to Pythagoras, that mystical demigod who began unlocking the secrets of the universe through mathematics. I want my students to see that with math it's possible to understand the universe, or at least explain part of it. It's because of Pythagoras and his followers that we have a better understanding of the stars, music, human life. I have one quotation underneath a large, elaborate sketch illustrating the harmony of the spheres, that reads: In numbers rather than in fire and earth and water the Pythagoreans thought they saw many likenesses to things that are, and that are coming to be, as for instance, JUSTICE is such a property of numbers, and SOUL and MIND are such properties, and another is OPPORTUNITY.

For the followers of Pythagoras, his theories became almost a religion. Marcoux's room offers nothing, and I want to blame everything that has happened with Sammy on this paltry room.

We stand to shake hands, agreeing that Sammy should apologize to the class with a written statement of his own, with which Anne and I are strongly encouraged to help.

Later in the day I'm back in my own classroom asking questions. Everyone seems a little distracted. Kirk Stout is quiet in the corner writing something to himself on the back of his notebook. Tedrick Jones, a handsome athletic boy, is flirting with Charlas Cain, the tallest girl in the school whose glorious afro adds another two inches to her height. Even Lan Nguyen's attention seems absorbed by something else, something not in this room, maybe the colors of the leaves on the maple tree just outside our window.

No one has offered a response to my question, so I call on Virginia Meyer, a bland nervous girl with stringy hair that is only sometimes washed, a mediocre student who sometimes knows the answers and sometimes doesn't. Today she doesn't have an answer, she says.

Normally, I let moments like this pass, glaze over them and move on to someone who might know the answer, or I work through the problem on the board with the class. But today, in response to Virginia's meek insufficient "I don't know," my pool of patience evaporates into a cloud.

"Why is it that you don't have an answer?" I say. I speak slowly and place large pauses between each sentence, getting more prickly with every word I utter. "Excuse me, but wasn't this part of the assignment for last night? I think it was. And because it was part of the assignment from last night, I expect that every person in here would have an answer, some kind of answer, a right answer or a wrong answer, but an answer just the same."

The heads of students slowly turn to the front of the classroom while I speak. Nobody says anything. Virginia's scalp becomes blotched with pink and red through her pale, dirty hair. I feel the heat rising from my neck to the tips of my ears. I'm confused. Everything is all mixed up, and I know I'll have to work extra hard now to remember exactly what I've asked.

At 6 pm, Anne is at her desk in the study, and Sammy sits in the big cushioned red chair on the other side of the room with his feet up on the ottoman reading his history book. He has a week to work on his apology, and Anne and I suggested he think about what he did over the next few days and we'll begin writing on the weekend.

When I say hello to them, they both say "hi" simultaneously into their books.

I thought marriage and children would teach me something, but I don't know anything that I can't carry with me in a backpack to and from school.

When I tell them I'm going out for a while, they both look at me, smile slightly, but don't say a word.

In the car, I pass through the best part of Rosedale Park out onto Outer Drive Road toward the freeway. Four blocks out, the houses change from well-kept Victorian and Gothic villas to tattered A-frames that look like they could blow away in the next strong wind. Once on the freeway, there's the bland comfort of concrete for a good twenty minutes until I pull off and park on Alberto's street in his neighborhood which sits in sight of the Ambassador Bridge. Leaves and litter gather in the crooks of porch steps and tree trunks. A woman talks to her boyfriend in Spanish and then switches to English when his friend, a tall man who is dark brown with a fine nose, comes walking over. She pouts out her lower lip and says, "MMMMMMYummmy Boy! You look like you in love!" They ignore me, kiss each other, and laugh.

Alberto answers the door wearing a white tee shirt and well worn blue jeans.

"My friend," he says and pulls me in with an arm around my shoulder. He's cooking and I watch him move around his small kitchen. Garlic and tomatoes simmer on the stove, and my saliva glands begin to swell. A dusting of flour and crumbs from a loaf of french bread, cut in half, covers the table near the window. The white and pink skins of garlic and onions are scattered among the yellow seeds from a green pepper. There are two wine glasses, empty, sitting beside the bread. I take the beer Alberto offers me.

"Have you lost your way home?" he asks. I want to talk to him about my life without seeming pathetic. I want to know how he stays in control. I want to be single again, and free. I want to bare my soul to someone, but I know that's more than just unattractive these days. I would like to be more modern about my life, my wife, my son -- wry, ironic, aloof, but I've never been any of those things. All the most modern moods feel like Halloween costumes on me. I look ridiculous in irony.

Before I have a chance to finish my dumb story about what the smell of garlic reminds me of, I hear a rap rap rap at the door. It's Julie carrying a bottle of wine. How nice, I think, like it's a chance party the universe has arranged for the three of us from some source of infinite wisdom. We can laugh all night.

But then I understand. We are no longer three; it's two plus one again. I'd like to say I turn them down when they offer to feed me. I stay for three hours, drink their wine and eat their food, and it is good.

When I get home, Anne and Sammy are sleeping. I lock up, check the doors, make sure that damned porch light is off. Anne turns the thermostat down to 65 degrees at night, and it's freezing when I walk up the stairs.

Sammy is a small thin bump under the otherwise unrumpled blankets. His room is extraordinarily neat. He's meticulous, insistent that every object has its own proper place. Even his backpack is carefully stowed in its own special spot on the shelf. This gift of extreme orderliness comes neither from Anne nor from me; it's all his own. He keeps the shade to his window up so the sun will wake him in the morning instead of an alarm clock.

His breath comes slow and even. Anything could happen. With the proper weight and pressure on the soft fluff of the pillow, I could smother my son. I could wake him up, hug him. I could tell him I love him, or, even though I know it's wrong, that I sometimes wish he had never been born. But I won't do any of these things tonight.

I move his microscope from its shelf, replace it with a coloring book, replace a model car on the other wall with the microscope, rest his bookbag in the opposite corner of the room on the floor.

From across the room I hear: "Dad? What are you doing?"

"Just straightening up," I tell him.

"Stop it," he says.

I walk over to the edge of his bed and sit down.

"Sam," I say. "Did you enjoy killing that hamster? Do you hurt things for the fun of it?"

Looking sleepy and a little afraid, he wraps his arms around my neck and begins to whimper into the shallow crevice between my shoulder and collarbone. His tears are real.

"Answer me," I say. But the more I insist, the harder he cries.

Even though it's dark, I know the leaves outside are still changing. Anne is asleep in the next room. I love my boy and we are all monstrous, aren't we?

Sammy sleeps without a pajama top, and he's shivering now. I slip the sheet and blankets back up over his shoulders and hold him tighter to make him stop crying. This is the only thing I know how to do. I keep him warm and pretend we're all safe.

GREAT ESCAPES FROM DETROIT

This morning when the phone rang I'd hoped it was the brown-eyed man with fleshy earlobes I had met last night at the Giacometti exhibit in the Boston Museum of Fine Art. He called himself Chas, short for Charles, but I overlooked that on account of the elegant curl of his upper lip over his straight teeth. I offered him my telephone number and an invitation to dinner.

Instead of Chas's eager acceptance of my dinner invitation on the other end of the telephone line, I heard my mother's bad-news voice say, "Peter." When everything is okay, she pronounces the t in my name as a soft, almost unspoken d. When there's trouble, I hear it in the sharp tick of her tongue against the roof of her mouth. She called to say that my cousin Alex died of a heroin overdose, in New York City. When I was an adolescent boy filled with wonder and anxiety, who couldn't accurately account for either, Alex was my best friend for a year; she came to live with us after her mother died. Her mother was my father's twin sister.

"The authorities said it was an accident," Mom said. "She'd just gotten out of rehab again. Probably wasn't used to her old dose." She paused. "She had my name and number listed at the rehab clinic as next of kin." She paused again. "After all this time."

Neither of us had seen nor heard from Alex in years.

"You okay?" my mother asked.

"I guess."

"Poor thing. It must have been a hard way to live."

"But a relatively easy way to die," I said. My mother sighed in agreement. At the other end of the line I heard water hitting the bottom of the porcelain sink in her basement studio. She was preparing a basin of water to soften the clay with which she makes decorative pottery to sell at arts and crafts fairs all around Michigan.

"How's the strip?" she said. I'm a cartoonist with a syndicated strip called "Stick-Figure Man." My mother once told me, in a fit of anger I incited, that very little else about my life has made her so proud.

"Fine," I said. "The strip is fine."

"Good," she said.

I'm often not as generous as I'd like when I talk to my mother on the telephone, and even when I want to say more, I have a hard time generating words to fill the seven or eight hundred miles of space between us. "Her boyfriend has AIDS," she finally said. "Can you believe it? After all this time? Almost a million people died of it in 2017. I looked it up." The long pause that followed wasn't an attempt to create drama; she simply didn't know what to say next.

I have a theory that my mother is always a little surprised that I'm a gay man in my thirties who still doesn't have either AIDS or a steady boyfriend. My guess is she's certain AIDS will be my end, rather than the more likely one I imagine: the hereditary brain tumor (astrocytoma they call it, a star of derangement expanding under the skull) that killed my father, Alex's mother, and their father before them.

"I'm negative, Mom," I said.

"Good," she said, and just when I thought I had overstepped my bounds again and embarrassed her, she added, "Me too."

Bradley, my father, died when I was ten. His twin sister Viv, Alex's mother, died five years later, the summer before I entered tenth grade and Alex became a high school senior. It took Bradley only four and a half months to die. They cut out part of his brain before administering chemo and radiation. He drifted back and forth between misery and confusion, and then plunged quickly into semi-silence and partial paralysis as his tumor grew back to derange the signals that told his body how to function properly.

Although Bradley and Viv died of the same kind of tumor, their deaths were very different. Alex, then seventeen, had walked home in the late afternoon August sun after swimming at a friend's house to find Viv sleepy and confused, propped up in front of the piano. It was a Tuesday, so Alex knew Viv had no students for that day, and it was unusual for her to be sitting at the piano that late in the afternoon when she normally napped before going in to the piano bar in Palmer Park, where she played and sometimes sang. Viv didn't recognize Alex. She plunked down the piano keys like a chimpanzee in a circus act. When Alex called her name, Viv's eyes rolled up until her irises disappeared and she lay back on the piano bench, her body shaking like a dropped and abandoned wind-up doll. Viv's shaking became more and more violent, and by the time she fell off the bench, her hair, shoulder-length auburn curls, had tangled into a web across her face. Then her body relaxed. She lay still for a few seconds before she sat up to see Alex crying. She said she felt fine, and asked what had happened? Viv refused to go to the emergency room, but arranged to see a doctor very soon after the seizure. On the afternoon of the doctor's appointment, Alex heard the car pull into the driveway, and waited for Viv to come in. Viv didn't come. Alex thought maybe Viv had stopped to talk to a neighbor, but after about fifteen minutes, she went out onto the porch to look for her. Alex found Viv dead near the bushes in front of the house, Viv's beige silk blouse and powder blue skirt stained by the grass on which she had thrashed about, her tongue bit clean through, the tip, looking like raw hamburger, lay on the ground next to her ear. They discovered the tumor on the autopsy.

Alex was, like her mother Viv, calm as the eye of a hurricane. Calm people worried my mother; she felt they didn't respect danger. If Mom found out Alex had been driving a friend's car without a license, or that I had to work a power saw in wood shop, she'd list the many types of disasters just waiting to happen, detailing the ease with which limbs and other appendages can be snapped off, or skulls crushed, or other horrific bodily injury inflicted. My mother was most in her element when describing the disasters that bloomed in her imagination, and for me it was like listening to a siren's song: horrible, yet inescapably compelling. I had grown used to these extended warning threnodies. Alex, having visited us often as a child, had heard my mother's lamentations of imagined dangers, but apparently hadn't realized the frequency or the intensity with which they were delivered until she moved in with us. Alex was more amused by these sessions than I, who secretly took them to heart.

Before my mother could get on a roll, Alex would try to head her off by saying, in her low even voice, "Aunt Jane. Relaaax." Commands to relax worked as well on my mother as they would on Hoover Dam. My mother courted solidity the way Viv had courted adventure, and the difference between the two approaches to living was most apparent in their offspring. I adored Alex as much as I feared her.

Instead of saying "Goodbye" to us as we left the house every morning, my mother would yell, "Be careful!" The muscles in my neck, shoulders and back tightened into knotty lumps, while Alex only waved goodbye and ran her fingers through her freshly washed hair to make sure it dried without a tangle.

We walked the two miles to school every day through our neighborhood. The colors of the slate tiled houses had been washed out by years of sun and the sooty kind of rain that only an industrial city like Detroit can produce. Our Detroit neighborhood couldn't compare with the distant suburb from which Alex had to move, but it was all we could offer. The houses with even less character than ours sported drab, dirty-white aluminum siding. There were blocks on which every fourth or fifth house had been abandoned or burned down. Even Alex, daring as she was, didn't linger on these blocks. On the other side of a business district's collection of auto repair shops, party stores, and gas stations, a more grand neighborhood called Shutterfield Green surrounded our school. Shutterfield Green houses were similar to each other only in their grandness, many of them three stories high, made of brick or stone and decorated with elaborate arches and pillars.

On that first school day in September, we reached the initial block of houses in Shutterfield Green, where lush lawns seemed to stretch a mile from sidewalk to porch, and Alex turned to face me. "Have you ever tasted buffalo meat? It's quite good," she said. "Much more savory than cow."

Who was this girl? Buffalo meat?

There was nothing I could find that was really wrong with Alex, but I knew that in my high school there was a fine line between eccentrically interesting and creepily untouchable, and since I often felt I fell on the wrong side of that line, I had little faith in my own powers of discernment.

Small breasted and all-over thin, the only thing that saved Alex from "skinny" were her shapely hips, from which her faded Levis, or the Scottish tartan skirts she took to wearing later, hung. She never took on the sloop-shouldered, arms-folded-in-front affectation of many girls her age, which made them look as if they needed either protection from a big strong man, or a new winter coat. Alex had the fierce posture of a queen governing a peaceful state.

Also unlike other girls her age, Alex used her eyes for emphasis rather than her hair. Under her left eye, near the bridge of her nose, a faint, crescent shaped scar hung on her otherwise unblemished face. This scar lent a strange intensity to her gaze whenever she looked anyone directly in the eye, which was all the time.

Over the next few weeks my anxieties about Alex waned. She was funny, daring, and smart enough to fit in anywhere. Her most odd attribute was that she seemed to really like me, even beyond the perfunctory way family must like one of their own. Alex showed me off to her new friends. "This is my cousin," she would say, "look at this!" She'd grab my notebook from underneath my arm and flip past the pages with notes on them to show her friends my drawings and sketches depicting the disasters my mother predicted for us: Alex in a car waving, her careering trajectory off an overpass, the horrible crash; me losing a finger in a saw, getting sucked in to lose my hand, my arm, until finally my head is sawed open to reveal the ants and worms of my brains. One of her friends was the journalism teacher's aide, and I credit Alex for getting me my first comic strip job on the school newspaper. In my beginning efforts at the strip, I showed the school mascot—a cobra—slithering around an athletic event spurting venomously clever barbs about the other team. Sometimes, just for the fun of it, I showed the cobra getting his head crushed by a Mack truck or a very large sneaker, just to keep him humble.

So I entertained Alex with my cartoons, and she entertained me with stories Viv had told her of my father and their life growing up together in Huron County, located at about the thumbnail of Michigan's thumb. I lacked the courage to tell her the only story I had heard about Viv.

When I was very young, five or six years old, I first asked why Alex had no father. My mother, who sat at her potting wheel in the basement, said only, "Some people just don't have fathers." I waited for something more. A year prior, my father had converted the basement into a roughly equipped pottery for my mother, and these were the days when my mother's forays into potting yielded far more failures than successes. The shelves were lined with crooked pots, and clay dust, and large warped bowls that my mother couldn't yet bear to throw away. When I asked my mother the question about Alex's father, she was having difficulty centering a slab of clay on the wheel, and I watched as the wet clay oozed like gray milk between her fingers. She removed her cupped hands from around the lump, and let it spin. The whole thing began to wobble again, and when she looked at me and sighed like it was the last breath she'd ever take I understood she wasn't going to elaborate about Alex's having no father. I knew not to ask again.

But I was a sponge for information I was not supposed to know. Sometimes, if I was especially tired from playing all day in the alley behind our house building forts inside abandoned cardboard boxes, or if it was a really good day and no one threatened to kick my ass or plant my face in the dirt, then I was exhausted and quiet at dinner and my parents would talk to each other, and almost forget I was there. This is how I learned that Viv had gotten the nickname "Running Bear" in the small town where they grew up. To a five year old most adult conversation is cryptic, and since I couldn't even spell yet I didn't understand that I had thought of the furry kind of "bear" instead of the naked kind of "bare" until I heard my mother say, in response to the news that Ralph Phelan had died, "January's a cold month to run naked through the streets. Poor Delia. It's a wonder she didn't turn that shotgun on Ralph."

"She didn't, though," my father said. "They stayed together until the day he died."

"But nothing really changed, did it?"

"Except that Delia never caught him again. Or, if she did, at least it wasn't at home in their own bed with the shotgun propped up in the corner of a closet."

They had a nice little laugh together over that.

"Well… Viv learned her lesson," said my mother. They both chuckled briefly, then, after a long pause between the two of them that felt to me like they were still talking to each other without words, my mother said, "A lesson."

Many years and other half-uttered aspersions on Viv's character passed before I fully understood my parents' reservations about the freeness with which Viv bestowed her affections on men. Even the liberties Viv gave Alex irked my mother, small things like the fact that Viv insisted on being called Viv instead of Mom.

Maybe it was because of my mother's prudery or because she didn't want to cause Alex more pain by reminding her she was now a true orphan, but I only heard my mother speak to Alex about Viv one time after Alex moved in with us. We were preparing dinner, and even then it was Alex who initiated the conversation. In the center of our kitchen stood a three foot by three foot wooden block on which my mother chopped anything that needed chopping: vegetables, clay, animal parts. That night it was salad. With one hand on the knife handle and the other on the dull side of the blade she leaned down onto a head of lettuce with all her weight and cut it swiftly into twos, fours, pieces, chunks, and bits, plucked out the unsavory parts and swept the rest into a large wooden bowl. Tomatoes and celery underwent similar swift dispatches. With radishes, she sat on her high wooden stool with a paring knife carving intricate shapes, always looking for new patterns of red and white.

Alex had been living with us for a little over a month. She finally mustered the strength to unpack the one carton of pictures and other valuables she'd brought with her from the house in which she and Viv had lived. Earlier in the day, Alex and I had collected all the pictures of Viv we could find, most of which were taken when Viv was just a girl. We showed my mother the pictures, and asked if she knew the stories behind them. "Looks like first communion," she'd say, or "I don't know," or "Prom? Did they have a prom? I'm not sure."

Finally, in frustration with herself and us, she put the vinegar and oil in a Mason jar with some minced garlic and shook it petulantly saying, "I don't have any stories. They were the storytellers, not me."

Every weekend, my mother packed our light green Chevy station wagon with her pottery, four card tables, and three folding chairs as we headed out to another craft fair somewhere, a tattered road atlas and the dog-eared

"Great Escapes from Detroit" as her guide to the artsiest fartsiest boondocks of the Great Lakes region, although we stayed mostly in Michigan. She padded the bed of the wagon with quilts, and packed cardboard boxes with old shirts, towels, and newspaper to keep the pottery from breaking. To pass the time, sometimes we played games like what famous person has these initials, or the song game, where one person sang as much of a song as they knew and the next person had to jump in with a different song that contained one word in common with the previous song. We sang a lot of love songs that year. The only time Alex seemed the least bit vulnerable to me was when she sang. Her speaking voice was low, but when she sang her voice went high, unsteady and quiet, and her face and neck blotched red. Sometimes, after we had exhausted our interest in games and each other, we just listened to the radio and watched the land tick by, waiting for a farmhouse, or a barn, or a stable of horses or some cows to divert us for a little while longer. While my father and Viv had grown up in rural communities, much like those we drove past on our weekend excursions, my mother had grown up in the city on the east side of Detroit. These drives seemed to be as new and exciting for her as they were for us.

Many of the craft fairs took place in large barns on failing farms where the farmers made money from billboards that stood in their fields among the crows and the livestock, and by renting barn space for crafts fairs.

It was first come, first served as far as booth position went at these fairs. Homemade rag dolls, different shapes of wood on which pink and white flowers had been painted, beanbags in the shapes of chickens that were sold as doorstops, or polished stones threaded with leather string comprised the majority of wares. My mother liked to jockey her booth closer to the arts than the crafts booths, if she could.

Some of the vendors traveled from show to show throughout the state as we did, and a little community of sorts formed among them, but I took my cues from Mom; we never extended ourselves. We smiled at them politely, and left it at that.

Alex talked to strangers.

Restless, she would wander through the crowd making friends and bring people back to our booth to talk, and they almost always bought something. Because most of the fairs were held in rural areas, a good many customers had lost limbs in accidents involving farm or mill machinery. One Saturday, during a fair in a town up near the rim of Saginaw Bay, Alex brought a one-armed woman named Eunice to our table. Alex had a peculiar fascination with the limbless and the torn because in place of a missing appendage there was usually a story.

Eunice, we found out, had not lost her arm working farm machinery. When she was a young girl, she had chased her younger brother near the barn. She was fond, at that time, of tickling him until he peed his pants. She had almost caught him near the barn, but as he ran, he bumped the rifle that their father had propped up against the trough. The rifle fell, discharged, and blew off Eunice's arm. "Oh," she said, "it was so long ago, I was only nine. I was in and out of it for a while. Yes, sure, it hurt very much. Phantom pain they called it, but it was real enough to me. Ha! Sure, but I got to eat a lot of pie after that for a long time. I s'pose if I'd not got injured I wouldn't be so fat," and she slapped her slightly round rump very hard with the flat of her remaining hand, laughed, bought one large flower pot and a set of four yellow bowls, and Alex helped carry them out to her truck.

The same day we met Eunice, Alex had nodded toward a booth across from ours, where two men had set up a display of their paintings and sculptures. The placard on their table read "Ernesto Sampras and Sam Day, Artisans. Petoskey, Michigan" printed neatly with purple paint on lime green paper. My mother and I saw Ernesto and Sam less frequently than we saw other vendors, maybe only three or four times a year.

Sam seemed to be in his mid thirties, had short sandy hair, a brown, closely trimmed beard and mustache, and always wore a flannel shirt. Ernesto looked to be late twenties, dark and lithe, and spoke with a Spanish accent. When he and Sam looked at each other my throat closed with what I had wished could have been disgust, but I knew it was envy.

"I wonder what their story is," Alex said, to which my mother quickly replied, "Alex, don't be so nosey. Stop approaching strangers and asking them personal questions." My mother settled back in her chair with a look of tight-lipped confusion. She leaned in closer to Alex. "You don't know what their home lives are like," she whispered. "And besides that, it's rude to pry."

"But they want to talk. People like it when someone shows an interest. They like telling their stories."

"But I don't like it," my mother said. "We make these trips to work, not to socialize."

We did not want their story. My mother and I had always kept our distance from Ernesto and Sam, and averted our gazes. It was safer, an unspoken pact, that we would continue to greet them, if at all, with only the most cursory forms of recognition.

Like any awkward teenager with budding creative urges, I began to assimilate whatever new thing I encountered into my cartoon strip to add any touch of exoticism I could muster in such a drab city as Detroit. After the first time I saw the Ambassador Bridge I had to restrain myself from including it in every single installment of the school strip, which I came to call "The Adventures of the Derring-Do Duo." And would it surprise anybody to learn that neither Alex nor I spoke about the fact that we never showed my mother any more of my strip after I created the Derring-Do Duo, two handsome, flannel-shirted, muscle laden men who bore a remarkable resemblance to Sam and Ernesto? I still drew the cobra occasionally, but more often the detailed drawings of the handsome Derring-Do Duo rescued an anonymous and unidentifiable character, Stick-Figure Man, from many kinds of peril. This was the crude birth of the character who later dominated my mind so much he became the basis for my syndicated strip.

That first glimpse of the bridge was an adventure in itself. Because Alex had never bothered to get her driver's license, my mother sold Viv's car along with the house and all the belongings Alex did not want, and put the money into a college fund account that Alex couldn't touch until she turned eighteen. I had gotten my license, but my mother rarely let me take the car alone until Alex arrived and convinced her that I'd forget how to drive if I didn't practice. We promised to take only the safest routes, even if it might take us longer to get where we were going.

So one day we borrowed my mother's car. We were supposed to drive to the store to get new jeans, but once out of the driveway, Alex decided that maybe we should go to Canada to shop instead of to one of the suburban malls. Alex navigated using the road atlas my mother kept in the back seat, and before I knew it I was queasy with fear and we were driving over the Ambassador Bridge. I was sure the border guards would pull us over and punish us, until Alex reminded me we weren't doing anything illegal. I was better on the way back, and after that all my cartoons involved the Derring-Do Duo rescuing the Stick-Figure Man dangling, or jumping, or climbing the Ambassador Bridge to escape another of Miss Hodge's English Lit exams by trying to escape to Canada.

Alex fed my fascination with bridges by telling me, one cold December morning on our way to school, how my father jumped off a bridge above a river to scare and impress girls when he was my age. Alex said that Viv had told her this story many times, and couldn't believe I had never heard it. "Hmmpph," she said.

"Anyway. He knew the bridge had a hidden ledge below it," she said, "and he knew how to jump off the stone wall of the bridge to make it look deadly. He'd take a girl walking through the park by the river where, in the autumn, the leaves of oaks and maples burned yellow and red. If things went well, they'd veer to the woods."

When she said, "things went well," I shivered at what this phrase suggested. Was this turn into the woods an innocent tromp through the leaves, or was there a more lurid aspect to my father I'd never suspected? Did they head for the cover of foliage so he could steal a kiss? To find out what color underwear she wore? Or maybe to taste her skin, move their bodies together and shake the leaves from the trees?

Sue Early was one of Viv's friends and also one of Bradley's "girls." Sue told Viv that when Bradley went walking with her, they started out at the park as innocently as if they were walking to church on separate sides of the street. He talked with Sue about the sorts of knots he tied on the farm, with rope the color of her hair, except that her hair was much nicer, softer, more glossy. From between her collarbone and her ear he chose a lock to roll between his forefinger and his thumb to make sure that, yes, her hair was very soft. A five minute walk down a path through a stand of trees led them to the chest-high stone wall they called "the bridge" simply because it bordered the river. Alex said, "Viv told me it wasn't really a bridge at all. More of a promontory with a wall." The look on her face turned dreamy. Her fingers stroked the tan suede fringe that hung from the arms of her jacket. "But we'll call it the bridge too. It's easier."

Promontory. I made a note to look the word up later. We were more than half way to school. I slowed my pace a little, wanting to hear the whole story.

At the wall atop the precipice, Bradley drew Sue's attention to the sounds of the sluice in the river below, where, he explained, great boulders narrowed the passage of water near the shore before the riverbed dropped to a grave depth, just a few feet out from the bridge. "Listen," he said. He began to sway, and then to dance. "I'm happy to be here with you," he said, his feet rubbing swiftly over the rough gray slabs of stone. "You're beautiful." Clomp, clomp, his heels came down hard when he spoke. "I could explode," he whispered. He leaned in, almost close enough to kiss her, then, when he sensed her heat coming forward, he pulled back quickly and hefted himself in one athletic leap onto the thin stone mantel of the wall. He danced a few more steps, made sure to catch her eye, hold the gaze, then: whoosh. Gone.

I've seen pictures of my father at that age: dark hair, dark eyes, a little on the short side, but strong, confident, lean with a face full of mischief and humor in equal proportions.

Sue ran to the edge screaming his name: "Bradley!"

Is that what my father sought? To hear his name spoken with such passion from the deepest part of the throat? Or maybe it was her face—the expression of panic and anger at having lost this sweet, dancing, dark-eyed boy. I imagined, from my father's vantage, dozens of girls in separate instances, each with ten delicate fingers grabbing onto hard stone, extending a head over the stone lip looking down to see... what? A body falling? A violent splash? The rippling water explode with the last air bubbles rising from Bradley's lungs? No. Her face hovers in the air above him to see Bradley, unimperiled, crouched and laughing on the ledge below looking up to savor her face in a pure state, smoothed out in panic or wide-eyed confusion, just before he stands up straight, says "hello," and kisses her, one hand hanging on to the ledge, the other caressing the back of her neck, warm under her hair.

"Something would change in every girl at the moment just before the kiss," Viv told Alex, and it was this alloy of emotion that my father worked with the skill of a silver smith. "Despicable," Viv had said to Alex, "but wonderful, huh?"

Or so the story goes, as told through Viv to Alex to me, the first male to hear this version. How strange, what women can tell each other that they can't tell men. This was a mother to daughter story, a story suggesting that the craftiness of men must be appreciated and sometimes rewarded, but also a warning not to be outwitted. It wasn't sex Viv warned against. She seemed to have counted on the fact that boys will try to have sex with girls. The threat lay in the way a sense of danger can heighten sex to the point where you might even believe it's love.

A week after the jumping incident with Sue, Viv said that Bradley pulled the same stunt with another girl, and many others after that. Sue, who was a bit high-strung anyway, found out about it, dropped out of school for a week, and often cried in class when she did come back. "Oh, she was crazy in love with him," Viv had said. Sue finished the year thin and pale, and finally recovered, but slowly. "And all because of a boy," Viv told Alex. "Silly, no?"

The smells of the moldy dirt and the tangy grass of our high school's football field, and the sight of the high steel cyclone fence surrounding it pulled me back into the gawky discomfort of my version of a fifteen year old boy: confused, unnatural, depraved. At the concrete steps in front of school, Alex said goodbye and headed for her first class. I forged my way through crowds of broad shouldered boys, girls blowing smoke rings in the early morning air, boys with strong limbs and sure movements who could move past another body as if it weren't even there.

Viv's lesson was this: do not to get too caught up in love. It can ruin you.

"Crazy in love," is an expression I'd often heard. Of this, at least, I knew I was in no danger.

With brain cancer, you expect derangement. I expected my father's to take the shape of the only kind of derangement I knew. Among my first blips and globs of memory, I see my mother's Uncle Denny in the throes of what I later came to understand as delirium tremens. Of course, I'm sure I've conflated parts of that story as told to me by my parents with the rudiments of my memory, but the whole of it formed like this: My father locked me in my room, which I know was blue, when Denny asked him how all those squirrels could live in the floor boards of our house. I tried to get back out into the living room to see what Denny was talking about, but the cut glass doorknob wouldn't move. By the time he began to scream, I knew something was wrong with Uncle Denny. I leaned my head against my hands on the bedroom wall near the door, listened and looked down at my red sneakers, the brown wood of the floor, the dark blue of the baseboard, and the lighter blue of the wall as Denny begged my father to get the squirrels away, to please make them stop scrambling up his legs to nibble at his nuts.

My father's dementia took a stranger, more calm turn. He died in winter. I was ten. For weeks he'd stare out the window while it snowed, not responding when my mother called his name. If he spoke at all, it was only to utter odd names for snowflakes: speariform, inverted spire, encrusted globule, asterisk, star of the sky, white demon.

On the days when no snow fell, he'd give himself over fully to sobbing grief. Speech had, near the end, gone completely, and all he produced from then on was excrement and tears. But we were lucky. That was a good winter with record snowfalls, during which we'd square his wheelchair against the window and pad his legs and stomach with hot water bottles, then tuck six or seven cotton quilts or wool blankets over his legs, under his neck, around his shoulders. And finally he'd grow silent again, his world filling up with whiteness, and he'd watch it fall.

I'm aware of the dangers inherent in the impulse to construct the dying father hero image toward which a boy of ten is prone. But that didn't happen until Alex came to live with us, five years after my father's death. Before Alex, the dominant perception that I held of my father involved the conglomerate stink of English Leather

cologne and talcum and shit and unhealed sores—a
steady, putrid smell that clubbed me with nausea.

My mother kept me home from school to help her; it
seemed to me she washed a load of laundry every hour.
She made me sit in that room every day waiting for
my father to die. I knew my grandfather had died the
same way, so I had an idea this was contagious. I tried
to breathe as little as possible while I was in the room.

It was February, the middle of winter, the day he died.
After the undertaker came for his body, Mom washed his
bedclothes and I scrubbed the bed and all the floors of
the house with Lysol and Murphy's Oil Soap. I marched
around the house opening all the windows and doors
to get the stink out at last. The cold air rushed in and
spread itself around until there was no corner of the
house where I couldn't stand and smell only cold pine
branches on inhalation, and on exhalation turn my breath
into a white stream that hung, spread, and finally disappeared. I'd never known such relief. I had wished that
could happen every day of my life.

It was the time of year after the ice has formed layer on
layer upon itself, and just before it breaks; when the days
are dark, and the nights are darker still, and longer; when
loss feels a part of every movement and you don't know
for sure if you can stand it: that's when Alex found a
boyfriend, and I began to feel the first slip of my tenuous
grip on her. She came less often on our weekend car
trips, and when she did come, Tim McCoarghty, her
new boyfriend, joined us and kept her mostly to himself.

I held nothing against Tim except his extreme good looks. He was quiet, but powerfully funny. He wore his reddish-brown hair long, and had calm, intelligent toffee-brown eyes. His lower lip was a bit fuller than his upper lip, which may have accounted for the slight speech impediment that put a burr at the end of the d, t, and s sounds when he spoke. Of red-haired people, I have found only two categories: strangely attractive, or plainly ugly. Tim was a marvel. I worked hard to keep from staring at him. Sometimes he would put gel in his hair, make it stand up like the branches of a dead tree, sometimes he'd comb it straight back, and other times he'd let it fall limp over his face and neck, as relaxed as his eyes. My anger and confusion at that period was unfocused; it swirled around a raging jealousy and was propelled by a desire for an unnamed and maddeningly unidentifiable something. I never knew if I was jealous of Tim for luring Alex away from us, or of Alex for having someone as cool and marvelous as Tim to leave us for.

On one of our last car trips where Alex and Tim accompanied us, it must have been in March, we drove up to Bad Axe, Michigan, the small town where Bradley and Viv grew up. I had never been there before, having had no reason to go since my grandparents had died before I was born, and the friends my father kept from childhood had all moved on to larger cities like Grand Rapids, or Lansing, or Traverse City. Mostly, I wanted to see the river where my father wooed and won women. Maybe, I remember thinking, the waters there could work a miracle for me, a secular sort of Lourdes that could calm and heal perversions like mine, turn my desire into something clean and fun, the way it sounded in other people's stories.

But there was no river that I could see from the highway, only the flat land of frozen fields. I couldn't ask my mother to find it, the spot where my father made mischief with other women. We did take a side trip to see the land on which Bradley and Viv had grown up. Where once there had been a farm, now there stood a large lot filled with tractors, combines and other farm equipment for sale. I could imagine nothing in that gravel lot other than the way it looked at that moment, so instead I looked at the patch of sky above the spot to imagine how the light might have shone on my father on a late winter day in March. I paid close attention as we pulled away and headed back toward the crafts fair. Dirt roads, wooden posts strung with wire to make a fence, field upon field upon field. Still no river.

The Bad Axe Antiques Mall, where the crafts fair was being held, was a long, narrow one-story building layered on the outside with corrugated sheet metal that had been painted olive. We'd gotten there late, and so had to set our booth near the end of the long corridor of booths. Tim and Alex helped set up, but neither could lift a pot or place a dish without touching the other in some way. Once my mother and I were settled into our folding chairs, Alex and Tim bantered and jostled, kissed and fondled each other constantly, which for me was an experience that wavered between titillation and disgust.

"It's unsightly," my mother finally told Alex when Tim excused himself to find a bathroom, "slobbering all over each other in public." I have tried to remember if I had ever seen my parents hug or kiss in front of me. I'm sure they must have, but I can't recall. I would hate to believe that in our family we did not risk affection.

Just before noon, we noticed someone setting up a new booth in the last available spot, a few spaces down and across from us. When Alex realized who it was, she said to me, "Where's Ernesto? Look, even their sign is different." It was a larger sign made with orange magic marker on white paper. It read "Sam Day, Painter. Lansing, Michigan." Sam had shaved off his beard and mustache, and I thought maybe that's why he looked thin and weary. His jeans sagged a little more than usual, and they looked like they could use a good washing. Even his hair looked thinner, and there was a fervent attentiveness about him that was disconcerting, as if his face had shrunk, or his eyes had grown.

The bathroom was located just past Sam's booth. After the third time I excused myself my mother asked me, "Are you all right?" I deflected as best I could, but I had to see what was up. I don't know what I expected to learn.

I had just sold a set of green and blue salt-glazed dinner plates to a short man with a rather square head, when a commotion began. Sam seemed to have made a mistake returning change to a customer. The customer, a very tall thin man with a deep voice, had bought a painting of a mustard field, and began to shout at Sam, "Are you trying to rip me off? I paid eighty dollars for that with a hundred dollar bill, and you give me back ten?" Sam fumbled through the bills he held in his hand. "I thought I...," he said. He looked at the bills in his hand, then at the bills in the red metal cash box. He shuffled the bills slowly, counting them, looked at the man, then back into his own hand. He sat down for a moment and said, "I'm sorry, sir. Wait a second," and gave the man two more ten-dollar bills.

"That's not right either," said the man. "What's wrong with you?" He threw one of the tens on the table, and as he walked off, the draft of air he left in his wake pulled the bill off the table and onto the floor. Instead of just bending over to pick the bill up, Sam knelt on both knees, then sat back on his heels and looked straight ahead of him. I hurried on to the bathroom. By the time I came back, Sam had returned to the chair behind his table. Except for my father, I have never seen such sadness on a man's face. He met my gaze and smiled shyly, but I looked quickly away, purposely avoided looking at him for the duration of the crafts fair, and I never saw him after that day. I still don't know the story of Ernesto and Sam, but I have made up twenty or fifty different versions for them, none of which could ever comfort me.

At our booth, Mom sat alone, stone-faced. "Where's Alex? I said.

"Off lolly-gagging someplace." She let out a snort. "Lost in love," she said, and rolled her eyes back until nothing showed but white.

Alex turned eighteen, received her inheritance, and left abruptly without much drama. She graduated high school and moved to New York. We heard from her often for the first month, then occasionally, and then almost never. She stopped returning calls, stopped answering letters, stopped sending cards at holidays, without any explanation.

I was very hurt, convinced I wasn't cool enough to capture or to keep Alex's attention. I knew she'd go on to do big, daring things, and that I'd be dogged by a constant need to avoid most kinds of danger, real or imagined. I hated myself for being such a white-washed bore, a stupendously careful coward.

I graduated from high school two years after Alex. I forced myself, although I was scared to death, to move to Boston to go to art school and to get away from the paralytic craving for safety I was sure my mother had cultivated in me. I blamed her for what we had most in common. I convinced myself that every move I made was daring and risky: moving away from home, going to art school, becoming a cartoonist. Only later did I realize that, in fact, everybody grows up and moves and works; it's totally unremarkable. Now I draw elaborate, opulently rendered worlds in which Stick-Figure Man has his adventures. I dismember him regularly, but, like a lizard, his stick-figure appendages always grow back. I always hoped that Alex would see my strip in a newspaper laying discarded on a table in a café somewhere and, voluntarily or not, think of me.

One time, after years of not hearing from her, we weren't even sure where she lived, Alex called me from rehab, the first time she went in. This was the first we heard of her heroin habit. She cried and cried and cried. She cried not because she needed something from me, specifically, but because she needed something, anything, that would make her less miserable. She called me again, just after she got out. "I'm on the straight and narrow," she said. "I still want it every day, but I guess I want to live more." We didn't have much to say after that because so much time had passed that we had few common experiences to discuss between us. I told her to keep in touch. That was five years ago, and the last time we spoke. I couldn't help her.

I suppose I shouldn't be relieved that Alex didn't die of a brain tumor, but I am, a little. I'm a year older than my father was when he died. Of course, I get a check-up every year to head off all kinds of corporeal disasters that may have bloomed in me without my knowledge or permission. Every year I outwit another kind of danger, or so I tell myself. It's much more satisfying to think that bad fortune can be held at bay through a force of will and health insurance, but even I know better than that.

After I hung up the phone with my mother this morning, I paced around my apartment trying to figure out what to do. There will be a memorial service in New York for Alex next week, arranged by her friends. My mother and I will both go. It'll be the first time I've seen Mom in about four months, since Christmas. We'll think about Alex the girl, hear stories from her friends about Alex the woman, whom neither of us knew.

And what about my mother? What are her stories? She lost her husband to cancer. She lost her spoiled, priggish son when he moved as far away from her as possible. And then she lost that same son again when she learned he'd never be someone she could think about without at least a degree of shame. When she found out I was gay, she told me, "I could have gone my whole life without knowing that. Let's pretend this conversation never took place." And so we did, for a long while. How could I have lived with someone for so long and still know so little about her? Sometimes, when she's really brave, she'll ask if I'm seeing someone. Oddly, this question always comes up just after I've broken off a relationship, no matter if it lasted a year or only a month. I had always interpreted her disappointment in my "no" as her general disappointment in me. But maybe I should give her more credit. Why wouldn't she want me to find someone to love, someone who could love me? Why wouldn't she want me to risk that, at least?

I made the arrangements for New York, and then debated whether I should call Chas, or wait for him to call me. My straight friends, most of whom are married, listen to me and gasp. "It brings back my worst memories of high school," they laugh. But I was too afraid of myself to date until I was almost thirty. All my high school memories are eclipsed by that one charmed year Alex came to stay with us.

Finally, I called Chas and made a date for dinner at a restaurant a few blocks away from my apartment in the South End. He said he was happy I called, that he was just getting up the nerve to call me himself.

I walk to the restaurant to meet him. It's a beautiful April evening, the magnolia trees are just beginning to bud. I'm a little excited and scared. Could he be the one? It's a pleasant thought, but so silly. I always feel foolish thinking it, but it still flashes through my mind.

I like to get to a date early so I can watch him walk toward me. The front windows of this restaurant extend from floor to ceiling. It's a little crowded tonight in the restaurant; I put my name in with the host and have a seat to watch the street. I was stood up once by a date. It's a horrible feeling, and ever since then I still always worry: Will he show?

Lots of people out tonight. Men and women walking in groups of two or three or four, couples holding hands, people alone or walking a dog. I spot Chas walking up the street. He's got good posture, and I love the way his arms swing when he walks, with no hint of affectation. His gait displays a comfort that borders on a galumph, which I like because it reminds me of his laugh last night when I met him, and how he made me laugh just by the slight crack in his voice when he said certain words. When he walks into the restaurant, I stand up and wait for him to see me. *Relaaax*, I think. The host seats a couple who have been waiting for a table. The line of vision between me and Chas opens; he smiles at me, and says my name, and I exhale through my smile.

Water glasses are packed with ice and filled before we even get to the table. He's sorry he's a little late, he says; I tell him no, I'm early. He tells me it's a comfort to meet someone as enthralled with Giacometti as he is. He says I'm cute. I'm still a little nervous, but who could dare ask for more? A cello suite is playing faintly overhead. The smells of baking bread, garlic, and tomatoes braid the air. A fresh miniature iris is in a thin vase on our table. I know this is our first date, we're not in love, and this may all come to nothing again, or it may turn into something much less than we'd hoped, or end in a disappointment neither of us could have guessed at. But maybe not. The water glasses have clouded over completely with condensation and begin to drip. *Encrusted globule, asterisk, star of the sky, constellate spasm.* I'm alive, and I know that the only real danger tonight is in not recognizing that in certain small moments life can be wholly beautiful.

LIVONIA

"Do a left, please, next light," Jeronimo told Claire. His high voice held a bird-like accent she couldn't place, in which he sang an extra vowel after the hard consonants at the ends of words. He was not from around here either. Claire wiped her palms (one at a time) on her jeans, gripped the steering wheel at ten and two.

"Don't worry," said Jeronimo.

"Don't-ah worry," repeated Claire. "Easy for you to say." She shocked herself with her imitation of his accent. She'd been trying for playful, not bitchy.

She pulled into the left turn lane, the light turned yellow and she stopped. Cars lined up behind her. A whirling congregation of crows fluttered down and perched in a row along the telephone wires under a sky so many shades of purplish gray it made Claire want to kiss someone.

Jacob. She wanted to kiss her neighbor's son, Jacob.

Claire shivered. In a borrowed car, on a busy five-lane road, in a nearly colorless suburb outside of Detroit called Livonia, in the middle of her thirty-sixth year, Claire Bonny, on edge and anxious learning to drive, did not think of kissing her husband or any of her three children. She wanted to kiss her neighbor's son, Jacob, who at the time was almost four years old, about the same age as Claire's middle child, Joseph.

"Hey," said Jeronimo. He reached over and lightly touched the pallid bumps of Claire's knuckles. "It's not that bad. Relax. Get into the middle of the intersection when the light changes, and when you see a chance, go."

Not-ah that-ah bad-uh, she sang in her head.

Oncoming traffic sped by, then cleared.

"Go," Jeronimo instructed.

Claire threaded past the cars, both parked and moving, in Livonia Mall's lot, and eased her way into one of the two spots marked with blue and white signs that said "E-Z Drive School." The school itself was a small office in a one story beige brick building filled with a strip of offices in the parking lot of the mall. The office smelled strongly of the brown synthetic carpeting that lined the floor. Claire had never seen any students other than herself enter or leave the school, or any teacher other than Jeronimo. The flier taped to the office window boasted that "highly trained driving instructors pick students up at their homes," but since Claire lived so close, she walked to her lessons.

From E-Z Drive she walked across the parking lot, crossed the five lanes of Seven Mile Road and trudged over the three sidewalk-less blocks home to see if her husband, Paul, had gotten up yet. It had been three days.

Her sons Robert and Joseph were awake and in the living room. Chad, the baby, still slept. Robert sat in what they called his bumping chair--a large, cushiony armchair in which he sat bumping his head and torso, moaning to hear the vibrato in his voice. Joseph sat on the living room carpet grinding his crayons down to nubs in one of his coloring books.

Claire poked her head into the bedroom where Paul lay staring at the ceiling.

"Hi," she said. "It's noon. I finished my lesson without killing anyone."

Paul's eyes moved to look at Claire's face rather than at the spot on the ceiling he'd been memorizing. Sometimes he tried to give a weak, fake smile, but this time he merely looked annoyed at having had his ceiling-staring marathon interrupted.

"Will you eat something?" she said.

He looked confused, and if a person could shrug from a supine position, she guessed that that was what he did.

Claire was a happy person. She couldn't help it. She'd known sadness, of course; it simply didn't stick to her. Disappointment, bad luck, severe grief at the death of her brother when she was sixteen and he seventeen--all these were real, but even severe grief softened, loosened and finally dissipated. She didn't know if it was a family defect or a gift: sadness for Claire and her family was like a drop of oil in a pool of water--a slick, slimy thing that may lay on the surface for a while, but never became a part of them. Eventually, sadness slid away.

Her father's remedy for the most ordinary brands of sadness was peanut butter and jelly sandwiches with chicken noodle soup and a glass of milk. It had always worked for Claire, and while she was a very bright woman, she still had difficulty understanding there were depths of sadness nothing material could touch. She had no other remedies, so she made the soup and sandwich and left them on an aluminum TV tray next to the bed. "Please try," she said to Paul. "One bite, one spoonful, one sip of milk. At least. Okay?" She knew the tray and the food would be just where she left them, unchanged, six hours later.

The purplish gray cloud cover of the morning had blown away. The sun bloomed. The mid-July day was coming on hot. She stepped gingerly over the scattered layer of partially crushed Cheerios on the kitchen and living room floors.

She asked Robert, "You got breakfast for you and Joseph?"

He kept bumping his back against the chair, but stopped the trembling moan for a moment to rattle out over three bumps, "Y-e-s." His vibrating voice sounded mechanical.

"Good boy. You've been quiet for Daddy?"

"Y-e-s-M-o-m-m-y."

"Once I get Chad up and fed you want to go out and play in the pool?"

Robert stopped bumping and looked at Claire. He held both arms of the chair.

"Yes?" she said.

He nodded vigorously.

"Maybe you can pick up the Cheerios from the floor while I get Chad ready."

Robert quickly dropped to the floor and began picking up Cheerios one by one.

"Put them in a bowl," Claire said. She went to greet the baby, already standing up in the crib, poopy pants and all, nibbling on the railing. She leaned into the hall again to whisper loudly, "Robert?"

"What?" he whispered loudly back.

"Just put them in the bowl," she said in her normal voice. "Don't eat them."

It had been a hard, drab, unbeautiful winter, and Paul had had a few more episodes of what he called his "moods." Two or three times over the previous year he'd had Claire call the radio station to say he couldn't come to work. She rose at four-thirty every morning to work on the greeting cards she made and sold through the web site she'd designed. Paul's morning show started at six o'clock, so every morning she'd poked her head into the bedroom at five to see if this was the day Paul would rouse himself and make it into work. The first morning of this latest episode he'd managed a complete sentence; he lifted his rumpled head about half an inch off the pillow and said "Will you call the station for me, please?" Claire knew by the way that one sentence sapped all Paul's strength for the rest of the day that this one might be a long haul. The next morning he'd said, "Call, please?" and then this morning he'd only shook his head no. Claire told Clinton, the night time Cool Jazz Guy's sound tech, that Paul had the flu and, despite his growing history of debilitating moods, she still half-wondered if it might be true: a mood virus.

Paul blamed it on the weather, and this seemed plausible, to a point. There'd been no big weather this year, none of the dramatic blizzards or ice storms Claire had come to love since moving to Michigan from New York, only a persistent cold drizzle that wore down the stones and kept everybody inside. Paul's first bad episode in New York and his failed acting career had prompted their move to Livonia, and he'd been relatively mood-free for the first few years after. Paul's moods came and went more frequently now, but without strong correlation to specific situations. For the past month the weather had been beautiful.

The months of spring came with no discernible shift in the cold rain, and then, one day, summer arrived and stunned everyone. That first day brightened with such force that one imagined the grass being pulled longer as the evaporating mists rose from it. By the end of the first day even the grass at the base of the huge maple in Paul and Claire's backyard had dried, and Claire was able to sit there watching the kids clatter and totter among the twigs and the dead winter leaves ground to silt by the winter rains.

Then, one hot morning the week after Claire began driving lessons, Paul couldn't get out of bed again.

"It's not you," he kept telling Claire, when he spoke at all that first day.

"Your job? Should you think about finding a new job?" she asked him. Each day he shook his head to signify "no" more slowly than the day before.

"It has nothing to do with you," he told her now as he had told her in the past, so of course she suspected it had something to do with her. He kept apologizing, saying he was sorry, sorry, sorry over and over, not specifying why he was sorry except to repeat that he was worthless, until Claire was sick of it. She knew he wasn't worthless, why didn't he? He was so different from when they'd first met, when his capability, confidence, strength would have bordered on the obnoxious had not his tender, almost feminine charm mitigated any hint of arrogance.

They'd met in New York at a Fourth of July party that had begun in the early afternoon. Most people had gone out of town to the Hamptons or to Fire Island. The host lived in a studio apartment in a fifth floor walk-up in Midtown and had only a fan, so the room had quickly become close. They saw each other immediately. She was the skinny, hazel-eyed, dishwater blond in the poppy red cocktail dress. He was the lithe guy in the floppy bucket hat with easy, sleepy brown eyes and full, red, Russian lips who'd stopped singing the minute she walked into the room.

She stepped over to the sink filled with melting ice to look for a beer. Paul worked his way over next to her, dipped a celery stick into a thick white dip and, because he was watching Claire, spilled a huge glob of the dip onto his navy blue shirt. Claire immediately flicked it off with her finger, grabbed him by the buttoned front of his shirt and pulled him to the sink, where she rubbed a cloth with water over the stain. She curled her mouth and blew some strands of her straight, somewhat thin hair away from her face while she worked at the stain. "There," she'd said, still holding onto the front of his shirt. She flipped her hair out of her face with two strong jerks of her head, right and left. "My name's Claire," she gave a brief, brisk nod to the sink, "and there doesn't seem to be any beer left."

"We should go get some," he said. He took her hands from his shirt and held them. "Paul," he said "Paul Bonny."

They left the party together, and married within six months. Despite the surprises that come with getting to know a new lover, she felt she knew him, not just because they lived together and now had a history. It was that nonsensical illusion that is part of falling in love. You feel not just that you know this new person, but that you've always known each other, and you've only been lucky enough to finally meet just now; a little late, but better than never: Oh, THERE you are.

Only now, after six years, did she begin to feel that the person she thought she knew was fading, his solidity evaporating under a heat and pressure she couldn't sense and didn't comprehend. Where before he'd swagger through the house playing his guitar or accordion for her and the kids, or sit at the piano and belt, really belt, out a tune at parties and family gatherings with his strong beautiful voice, now he hunkered into the pillow and whispered meekly, "Please. I'm sorry. Don't tell Dad, okay? Or anyone. Please? I'm so sorry. But don't tell Dad."

She had promised not to say anything to his father, Jonathan, and Jonathan persistently pretended not to notice anything wrong. Jonathan normally babysat the kids on the mornings Claire took her driving lessons, but when Paul stayed home all he'd let her tell Jonathan was that he was under the weather again and they wouldn't need a sitter that morning. Jonathan never asked for more information.

As much as the situation strained Claire's belief in sadness without a cause, it also strained her patience. "The weather? The kids? Our life together?" It went like that, Claire asking questions, Paul trying to muster an answer for a while. It was like watching the batteries in a toy slowly wear down.

Every time Claire stepped into their big backyard she remembered this was one of the only consolations for moving from Manhattan, and she always took a moment to look around to appreciate it. A tall, skinny pine tree grew in one corner, and a mutant variety of maple--impossibly tall, leaves bigger than Claire's head--grew in the other corner. The maple's leaves were blue-green in summer, and when the chlorophyll ran out in the autumn... well, she just couldn't believe her luck. She could stare at that tree for hours and feel better in any weather. Even in winter, the complicated symmetry of its barren branches thrilled her. Now the light shot through the leaves to cast a pale umbrella of shade over one half of the yard, leaving plenty of sun for the kids to play in the white-yellow uncovered day that stretched through the other half, nearer the house.

Leaving Paul behind in their dark bedroom, Claire stepped out and felt the hot sting of the sun on her arms. Her three sons doddered lazily behind her. The kids' pool was already inflated. She dumped out the stale water, dragged it further into the yard away from the house, as if she really thought anything could disturb Paul's sleep.

Claire didn't admit to herself until the pool was almost filled that she was hoping Estelle's mother, Beauty, would come out into the yard next door with Jacob.

The water trembled through the narrow opening of the hose in Claire's hand, pushing and pulling in spurts and burps over the inflatable pool. Claire looked at her children. Three different children should have three different personalities, according to common wisdom. Her children couldn't be more alike: careful in everything, painfully shy, extremely well-behaved. They were lovable.

Yet she couldn't help but wonder: where was Jacob?

The pool filled. Claire's kids cautiously tested the water and squirmed at the coldness of it. They milled around the yard picking bugs off trees and off the cement driveway to play with them while they waited for the pool to warm. Claire set Chad in his walker and sat under the tree to read "Madame Bovary." At the descriptions of the dullness of Emma's days, Claire had just about had it, and thought "Good Christ, Emma, snap out of it!"

She laid the book against her stomach, and brushed her fingers over the hot grass to let the blades tickle her skin.

Where was Jacob?

Estelle and her son Jacob had moved in next to Claire and Paul in May, toward the end of the winterish spring. Beauty took care of Jacob while Estelle worked downtown as a secretary in the Classics Department at Wayne State University.

Unlike her mother, Estelle was open and friendly. She had the same wide, voluptuous mouth as Beauty, the same almond eyes and overly prominent nose, but she was softer. Estelle's skin tanned easily and her eyes were brown, where Beauty was quite fair with startling, almost creepy, light green eyes. Beauty had had her hair lightened, cut and shaped into a New England bob--a style she seemed to have chosen for the way it looked on other women she'd seen and admired, and not for the way it worked on her. The delicate cut around the face of a person with features as strong as Beauty's made her look misplaced, lopsided, even though the proportions were painfully exact. Estelle's chestnut hair fell freely over her shoulders and around her face as naturally as a stream runs over pebbles.

Claire's fantasy of the Midwest included making and presenting a warm cherry pie for the new neighbor. This was her first new neighbor opportunity, and even though nobody had brought her anything when she and Paul moved in, Claire took her chance. The third day after Estelle and Jacob moved in Claire spent all morning making the pie. When Paul came home that night, she left the kids with him and went over alone. She fell in love with Jacob immediately, but couldn't for the life of her say why. She watched him play by himself using pens and pencils as building blocks. He talked to himself the whole time, commenting on the buildings and what went on inside. She strained to listen, but Claire couldn't quite make out what he was saying. The expressions on his face, all his movements fascinated her. Jacob was vibrant! Colorful! Alive! Claire had to make an effort to pay attention to what Estelle said.

Jacob threw a tantrum when the ice cream truck came by and Estelle told him he couldn't have any because he hadn't eaten dinner yet. He stamped his feet, panted, and whimpered, and Claire loved him even more.

Claire's work painting and sketching images for the greeting cards she made and sold on the web site she'd designed had begun to bore her; she hadn't had any new ideas in months, even though she'd looked everywhere. She mostly drew people, or cartoon versions of people, her trademark characters drawn with a few deft strokes. One line slanted just the right way on a face could make all the difference. After having gone through a phase where she depicted odd plants and outdoor scenes, she sought inspiration in the shopping malls. When she had a chance she'd stroll the stroller through the mud and tracks of the subdivision over to Livonia Mall and sit watching a club of senior citizens and extraordinarily fat people make their mall-walking rounds. Sometimes she'd sketch a certain face, a posture, or gesture. She looked to her kids for ideas too, feeling guilty for not finding anything in their faces she could use.

The morning following Claire's first meeting with Estelle and Jacob, Claire woke at 4:30 AM to sketch Jacob's pout, and she nailed it. Then she did his look of curiosity: head tilted almost completely sideways, eyes squinting, squiggle of nose here, curl of mouth there. She thought about Jacob and everything she drew was good as gold.

It had been a month since that first meeting, a month of outrageous productivity for Claire. She hadn't had a period like this since just after she first met Paul. She got back her verve, plus some. Somehow Jacob stirred up everything she'd felt that first year with Paul. Just after she met Paul she started to work like a mule. She painted and drew everything she saw. Everything interested her, and everything she finished satisfied her. It was the same way with Jacob. If she could have, she'd have managed to see Jacob all day, every day. But Beauty scared her.

Two days after meeting Estelle, Claire met Beauty. It was only the second day of fine weather; the ground had hardly had time to fully thaw when Beauty began gardening in Estelle's yard. Beauty took off her bright blue gardening gloves and thrust out her hand to shake Claire's. "Name's Beauty. You can call me Bea. If you want." Beauty had upended the hoe and flicked off the half of a grub that had stuck there. She'd set the hoe right again, and said, "I prefer Beauty, but it makes some people uncomfortable." Then she'd pulled her gloves back on, walked away and began to tear open the lawn in a border about a foot away from the foundation of the house. In the month that had passed, big, dramatic flowers now shot up: snapdragons, gladiolas, hyacinths.

Every time Claire came out to the yard, Beauty took Jacob back inside. She doubted Beauty avoided her for any personal reason, and hoped she was just generally unfriendly. But today the weather seemed too fine to keep even Beauty inside just to avoid a neighbor. Claire relaxed, let the kids play while the sun warmed the pool water.

After about an hour, Beauty and Jacob marched into the backyard, each with a rake as tall as themselves. They proceeded to scour the lawn. Beauty scraped the ground with ferocity; Jacob lifted his rake high in the air, lowered it to the ground using his whole body and petted the grass with his rake as if it were a favorite giant animal on whose back he rode returning to his enchanted palace.

Jacob faced Claire's children, eyeing the pool.

Claire waved and smiled. Jacob straightened his back and waved. He was perfectly proportioned with dark brown eyes and light brown hair that was sure to be blond by summer's end. Claire walked to the fence to say hello.

"Hi," he answered. He was not shy. "How are you?" Claire, not used to being addressed in so forthright a manner from so young a child, laughed.

"Would you like to come swimming?" she asked.

Jacob nodded his head yes, then turned toward his grandmother whose cotton shirt was darkening in spots with her perspiration.

"Beauty," Claire called. Beauty turned her head, but did not stop raking. She nodded once, as a greeting, and continued her task.

"Beauty?" Claire called again. This time Beauty stopped and turned full around. She held the rake handle with both hands and walked over to the fence to take care of whatever business Claire was interrupting her work to discuss.

"I just thought Jacob might like to come over to play in the pool."

Beauty looked at the pool, then at Claire's kids in the pool, then back at Claire. Robert watched his hands as he slowly raised and lowered them in the water. Joseph leaned over the edge of the pool to stare at an ant crawling over the plastic rim.

"We're raking," Beauty said. "Thanks. Maybe some other time." She nodded at Jacob and said, "C'mon Jacob," but any fool could have guessed what was gathering in the quiet child's lungs.

"No!" he whined. "I want to go swimming."

"Jacob," said Beauty.

He began to pout, and Claire thought she'd never seen a more attractive child.

"I want to go swimming."

"Jacob," Beauty warned again. She lowered her head and looked at Jacob with eyes menacingly slid to the side of her sockets. The tantrum broke when she reached out her hand to take his.

He screamed, "NO! I want to go swimming." He hit the fence with the rake. Beauty lifted his arm, spanked his butt hard, and straightened while he wailed. She looked directly at Claire and clamped her lips together. Claire saw them quiver with the tension it took to keep them closed.

Jacob wrapped his soft hands around the wire of the cyclone fence that separated their yards and cried hard. Claire knelt to stroke his fingers with hers. "It's okay," she said. "We've got the whole summer." But he wailed louder.

"Beauty," Claire said, "Surely it couldn't hurt if he came for a little while. It's so hot. He'd have fun."

Beauty had already gone back to raking and Claire spoke to her back. The look on Beauty's face as she turned to present it to Claire could have felled a redwood. She marched over to Jacob, bent over at the hips, both hands on her straightened knees to position her face very close to his.

"Do you want me to give you something to cry about? Stop it!" She straightened a little, spanked him again, pried him loose from the fence, and forced the rake into his hands by bending his fingers one by one around the handle.

Claire's kids stared at Beauty. Beauty returned to raking, Jacob continued to wail, one hand on the fence, the other on the rake. Robert and Joseph's attentions returned to hands and ants, and Claire sat stroking Jacob's fingers through the wire fence.

Beauty finished scraping together a small pile of the scraps of grass and dirty twigs, shoved it all into a plastic bag, and did something Claire did not expect: she went into the house, slammed down all the windows one by one, and closed the doors.

The lock on Beauty's back door clicked, then the air conditioner in the back window screeched and began to whirr. Claire waited. Beauty didn't come back out. Jacob continued to cry. Once she was gone it seemed that Claire was the one denying him his bratty wish, and not Beauty.

He kept repeating, "I want to go swimming I want to go swimming I want to go swimming" continuously in gasping sobs that shook his whole body. At one point, after about the hundredth time he repeated the phrase, he lost his breath. "I want to go swim..." he stopped, gulped in three gasps of breath before he continued, "MMiiiiinnnng!" then followed it with plaintive sobs between his chants.

Claire felt like a monster. Paul lay in the bedroom prostrate. Beauty was not coming back out. Claire's kids were relatively happy, and Jacob wailed. Although she knew she shouldn't do it, she stood up.

"C'mon," she said. She motioned to Jacob over the fence. He lifted his hands above his head, and Claire hoisted him up and over the fence into her own backyard. She kissed his beautiful face and hugged him, rocking him in her arms. He buried his face in her neck and quieted. She thought Beauty might come back out, but she didn't. After a few minutes, she stripped off all Jacob's clothes, stripped the bathing suits off Robert and Joseph so Jacob wouldn't feel too different, stripped off Chad's diaper and propped him next to Robert, all in the pool together.

Her heart beat like a crazy woman's.

Her sons, in their usual fits of shyness, ignored Jacob. "Boys," Claire said, "This is Jacob. Jacob, this is Robert, Joseph, Chad. Robert, show Jacob how far you can squirt with the squirty duck."

Robert refused to look at Claire or at Jacob. Jacob stood, the three other boys sat.

"Hey," Claire said to Joseph. She splashed him a little, hoping he'd splash back, but he turned away and looked like he was going to cry.

Claire turned to look at Jacob. He looked directly at her. None of her sons ever did that with people they weren't familiar with. Jacob shrugged.

"Hey," she said, and splashed Jacob.

"Hey!" said Jacob. He kicked a wave at her. Her sons recoiled.

"Hey!" she said, and soaked Jacob, using both hands to splash him.

He replied, "Hey! Hey! Hey! Hey!" He kicked water and laughed.

Finally, when they saw Claire drenched and laughing, her sons joined in laughing and splashing until they'd splashed almost all the water out of the pool. After that, Claire decided to put the sprinkler on and let them run through it. Claire held both of Chad's hands and lifted him over the spray. He screamed with delight.

Claire managed to forget about Paul prostrate in bed and Beauty fuming in the air conditioning of the house next door. Claire was soaked, her hair dripping, her shorts and top becoming uncomfortable. She set up the umbrella with Chad underneath it on a blanket, then stretched out on a lawn chair pulled into the sun to dry herself off.

Jacob scrambled over to Claire in his funny, loping walk. He kicked out his legs and let his arms fly around to balance himself. He reached out for Chad by extending his two index fingers. Chad grabbed on and Jacob led him to the point midway between the sprinkler and the farthest point of the water's arc so that every half minute or so Jacob and Chad were sprinkled lightly, and Chad vibrated with joy. Jacob would duck as if in hiding, but when the stream reached them he'd stand and jump and raise his hands in the air as if to scare the water away, and Chad would clap and laugh.

From her spot in the sun, Claire saw a curtain in the air-conditioned room next door pulled aside, then dropped. A minute later she heard a screen door slam, and felt that familiar pang of love: happy the way she used to be happy after she'd first met Paul and didn't want to see him go for the day. Her heart beat right up into her throat as she waited for what would come next.

She knew she was wrong to ignore Beauty's discipline of Jacob, but she looked at Jacob and she wasn't sorry at all.

Beauty walked into the backyard. Claire ran over to the fence, her wet shorts sagging off her hips, her tee shirt plastered to her skin, mildly obscene, her hair dripping water like some shaggy animal, and tried to appear rational and persuasive.

She held her hands up in surrender and heard herself babble: "Look, I'm sorry, I shouldn't have usurped your authority, you're his grandmother, and I'd be angry if someone did that to me, but he looked so lonely and I wanted my kids to get to know him, it's good for kids to have friends, but it's totally my fault, not Jacob's, I lifted him over, I'm sorry."

She knew she looked hysterical, and knew there was very little chance of making the situation anything but an ugly scene. But Beauty surprised her again.

"Well," Beauty said. "As long as we agree." She lifted her chin and straightened her back. "Do we?"

"Do we...?" Claire was confused.

"Agree."

"Oh," said Claire. "Yes."

Beauty stood still for the first time Claire could remember. She crossed and then uncrossed her arms, and said, "I shouldn't've gone back into the house." It took her a long time to speak, as if she were typing the words out in her head before she uttered them. "Sometimes I get angry." She looked away, over the back fence at the house behind her daughter's. "Estelle will tell you."

They stood awkwardly for a moment before Beauty called out Jacob's name. And although she snapped her fingers for him to come, it was not an unkind gesture.

"You're not..." Claire said. She calculated how much more overstepping of boundaries Beauty would brook. "He's not.... I didn't get him into more trouble, did I?"

Jacob stood next to Claire with his underwear wadded in his hand. Instinctively, Claire picked him up. He clung to Claire, but looked at Beauty, completely unperturbed. He put a foot on the fence.

"You're not coming over that way," Beauty said. "Like some zoo animal. You can walk around, okay?"

"Okay," he said and scrambled down out of Claire's grip.

"After you put your underwear and shorts back on."

He did as he was told, all the while looking at Beauty. It was clear that he loved her. Finally, Beauty turned her attention back to Claire. "Jacob is a good boy," she said. "Often." She huffed out a little laugh.

She clucked her tongue once, and said to Jacob, "I'll meet you out front."

Jacob disappeared around the corner of Claire's house without giving her a second thought or saying goodbye, and for the first time in a very long time Claire thought that if she wasn't careful she might cry.

Estelle came home from work at four-thirty every evening. Beauty drove off in her old orange Dodge Dart at exactly five o'clock. Claire brought the boys out on the porch and knocked on Estelle's door as soon as she was sure Beauty was gone and wouldn't be coming back.

Estelle laughed the whole thing off. She told Claire her mother was a hard woman.

"Don't worry about my Mom. She's a bit of a cold fish. She's afraid people will find out about our 'secrets,' as if we have such important things to hide. She says I was born to spite her 'cause I'm such a blabbermouth. But really, who cares? Besides, if you can't talk to people for real why talk to people at all, you know?"

"Yes," Claire said quietly.

"Anyway. That's what happens when you're named after a horse," she said.

"A horse?"

"My grandfather was a circus horse trainer, Grandma was one of the very first woman clowns," Estelle told Claire. She paused as if she were processing the information anew. "In America, anyway. At least that's what Mom says." She closed her eyes and laughed softly before opening her eyes again. "For a while, Mom was the girl in the pink tutu who rode barefoot on the horse's back around the ring. Can you imagine?"

Claire's boys had lined up their model cars in neat rows on the porch. Still a bit leery of the newcomer, the boys kept their backs to Jacob. To give the kids room to play, Claire moved the lawn chairs off the porch and onto the front lawn while Estelle went inside to fetch a couple of beers for them.

"Mom is really great when she warms up. I guess it was hard for her." Estelle popped open a beer, handed it to Claire and settled into her chair. "When she was sixteen she ran away with an accountant who left her four months later. Four years went by that she won't talk about, then she met my father." She paused. "A weakling," Estelle said. She scratched her head with both hands, shook her hair, and leaned forward so that all her hair fell in front of her face, then flipped her head back and let her hair fall in a fresh wave over her shoulders.

"He committed suicide just after I started school. Second grade," she said. "Catholic school. Lucky me: My father, the mortal sinner," she laughed.

"But I'm no better than Mom," she added. "I'm the poster child for making the mistakes of the parent. I mean, Jacob's father didn't kill himself, but he's just as available as if he had. He's one of those Portuguese poets with the heavy eyelids and an insatiable libido." Estelle made a sleepy-eyed seductive pouty-lipped face. In a Portuguese accent, giving extra throat-scraping emphasis to the 'h' and the 'r' sounds, she said, "I am having a hard-on." They both laughed "We met at a writing workshop I went to in Prague when I was between semesters in grad school. We moved in together the first week." She twisted her mouth into a chagrinned grin. "Inseparable the whole summer."

The starlings of Livonia screeched as they gathered in an oak at the end of their block. Estelle appeared absorbed in that ordered chaos. She sipped her beer and laughed. "If I ever did write the story of my life, it'd be called 'My Life: The Cliché'. You've heard the story a thousand times. Intense young love, girl gets pregnant, man goes poof into thin air." With her beer can perched between her thighs, she lifted her palms and flexed her fingers up and out to exemplify "poof," then took another sip of beer.

This sudden outpouring of information stunned Claire. She felt an urge to reciprocate, to divulge a host of her own sadnesses--to talk about the death of her young brother so many years ago, the flat ugliness of Livonia compared to the towering beauty of Manhattan, the surprise she felt at her immense fear of driving, and, of course, Paul. But her urge to divulge was only an urge, and it passed quickly.

Claire sat quietly, lightly traced with her finger the corrugations on the aluminum handles of her lawn chair, and pretended to look at the starlings gathering at the end of the block in the oak against the darkening sky. It seemed rude not to respond to Estelle's family stories, but Claire couldn't think of anything to say. Neither "wow" nor "I'm sorry" seemed appropriate. She couldn't just launch into her current confusion about her long days worrying about Paul. Had Estelle asked about him, a simple comment perhaps, Haven't seen your husband around lately, Claire's thoughts may have made it all the way to speech. But she bored herself when she complained, and what would she say anyway? He's depressed. Had Estelle asked About what? Claire could have only said, Well, we don't know.

About a minute or so had passed with neither Claire nor Estelle speaking, and the discomfort between the two of them was growing. Claire could only guess which twitches of thought reached her face, and how Estelle might interpret them.

Jacob, testing the wheels on the Hotwheel cars, crashed one car into two others lined up at the edge of the porch, causing all three to sail into the bushes. Robert began to cry. By the time Claire and Estelle turned around, Jacob appeared to regret what he'd done and petted Robert on the shoulder. "It's okay," Jacob told him. "It's okay." Jacob scrambled off the porch and into the bushes. "See?" he said. He brought up each toy car along with a handful of dirt and placed them side by side onto the porch.

Claire said, "I love Jacob."

The discomfort between them fell away. The suburban dusk with its attendant phenomena of streetlights sputtering on, mosquitoes buzzing around juicy flesh, and the occasional blipping light of fireflies dancing over the lawns swaddled Claire and Estelle as they resumed speaking about nothing important at all in low, contented voices.

Parallel parking was a trial, but it didn't scare Claire. Driving above ten miles per hour scared Claire. Pulling out into the open road scared Claire more, almost as much as driving next to, or behind, or in front of another car scared Claire. But in the end, not being able to drive in case of an emergency scared Claire more.

She'd called the driving school about a month after Paul had fully recovered from his third debilitating mood. None of the episodes he'd had since they moved to Michigan lasted as long as the first one in New York, but each new one seemed to linger a little longer than the last. The first bedridden episode in Michigan ended after only two days. This fourth episode was approaching its second week.

How much had changed since they first met! Claire would have never imagined being in a position where she'd need to learn how to drive. She suspected that Jeronimo, her driving instructor, was a little afraid of her, but he was extremely patient.

"Uhmm," he'd say, "you might not want to go quite so slowly here. The speed limit is thirty-five, so if you got up to thirty, that would be good. Stay in the right lane. Good. Good. Little more gas." Then he'd exhale in a little whistle. "Very good, Claire. You're doing fine."

She thought it would be different. She thought she'd get in the car and just GO. In everything else she was a quick learner and fearless, but behind the wheel of a car she felt like a baby, squirming and about ready to scream.

"How do you know?" she asked Jeronimo. "How do you know what the speed limit is? I can never tell."

Jeronimo explained about the signs along the road, which Claire remembered seeing as a passenger, but as a driver there were so many other things to look out for.

"Probably I shouldn't say," Jeronimo hesitated. Claire loved hearing him say words ending in "d' and "t." I shouldn't-uh say. His voice was high, more than a bit feminine, and cracked frequently, which made everything he said sound a little like a joke. He told her, "Instead of thinking of the speed limit, think to keep pace with traffic. It's much easier. Stay behind the car ahead of you enough to safely stop in case of an emergency. Not that far, Claire. You can get a little closer. Good, that's fine. Don't worry about the speed limit."

By the third week of lessons Claire could keep up with traffic, and read the signs without too much extra effort. She still couldn't listen to the radio, but she began to talk.

"Are you married?" she asked Jeronimo. She had turned left off of Middlebelt onto Five Mile Road, and was headed east toward Detroit.

"No," he said. "Stay in the lane. Stay in the lane."

When she was terrified, Jeronimo was warm and friendly, talking all kinds of small talk to which she could never respond because if she spoke she'd lose her concentration, unconsciously ease her foot from the gas pedal, and veer out of her lane, especially if he asked a question. But even though she'd heard how driving lent itself to letting the mind wander, what would she tell him anyway? That lately she was preoccupied with the past? She'd never, even after her brother's death, looked back so much. She constantly caught herself as she retraced events to look for clues, which on retrospect were not subtle clues at all but bald warnings of the turbulence ahead for her. She wanted to tell Jeronimo about her first Thanksgiving in Livonia, just a few months after she and Paul met and decided to marry. That picture on the mantel alone should have given her pause.

It was a picture of Paul as a young boy that he claimed he didn't remember being taken. In fact, it was a rather generic picture of a boy; it could have been any boy in any backyard in any state launching an airplane from the depths of suburban domesticity into the wild blue yonder. Claire was struck by the intensity on the boy's face. It was the same intensity she'd fallen in love with in Paul the man, but in the picture she saw the danger of that intensity too. The boy in the picture didn't want to just launch that airplane; he looked like he'd run a mile to rev up and wanted that thing to fly past the edges of the earth and never come back. And although the intensity and concentration of his expression resembled anger, Claire found it beautiful, exquisite. "The Passion of Paul," she called the picture.

Paul's sister, Denise, home for Thanksgiving from Arizona, let it slip that the picture had been taken by Paul's mother, around the time of her first arrest for parading naked around the neighborhood asking neighbors, "Have you seen me?" Claire learned big facts about Paul's mother in clipped phrases and half sentences, beyond which neither Paul nor his family would elaborate: Mental institution after third lapse. Eloise. Died there. Chicken bone. Choked.

Could she tell Jeronimo these things? When she gained the proficiency to talk and drive at the same time, and began asking questions that concerned him and his life, he was neither warm nor forthcoming. But Claire persisted.

"Girlfriend?" she'd say.

"No. Stay in the lane. Keep your eye on the road."

Her life was in his hands. She didn't even know what country he came from.

"Jeronimo," she said. "What kind of name is Jeronimo?"

"You are going to do a turn around here," he said, "to get on to Telegraph, heading north. Turn right, then bear left, then turn around. Okay?" He guided her through the move, and once they were in fast traffic and Claire was keeping up without problems, she settled down and asked again.

"So, what kind of name is Jeronimo?"

"Stay in the lane," Jeronimo said. "Jeronimo. It was my grandfather's name."

"From?" she asked.

"From his father," said Jeronimo. "Stay in the lane."

"Oh," said Claire. She tried to think of another question to ask, but he made her do a loop-de-loop off Telegraph Road onto westbound Eight Mile, which involved completing several full circles, then merging into unbelievably heavy and fast traffic. Claire was too shaken to speak for the rest of the lesson, and at that point didn't give a damn if she knew any more about Jeronimo or not.

On the long tense ride back to Livonia Mall she thought again of Paul's mother, who she knew so little about.

On three separate occasions Claire had tried to steer a conversation toward the topic of Paul's mother, and each time the exact same thing happened. Jonathan, Paul's father, said, "She was a wonderful woman." The words sounded with the snap of someone putting the cap on a bottle. Denise and Paul clamped down accordingly. The starkness of the statement and the complete lack of subtlety with which the conversation was changed made it clear that certain topics in this family were not tolerated. Only once, walking the two blocks home from Jonathan's house, did Claire press Paul.

"Why won't anyone talk about your mom? I feel like I'm missing something."

"You know the expression, 'Why beat a dead horse?'" he asked.

"Yeah?"

"Same thing goes for dead mothers," Paul said. "No biggie. Let it go, Claire."

That first Thanksgiving one of the relatives commented how Denise looked so much like their mother it was frightening. "I got the looks," Denise joked. "Paul got everything else." The room laughed the way people laugh when they see someone slip on a patch of ice: nervous, ashamed, afraid, because they don't know what else to do.

It wouldn't matter if she told all this to Jeronimo. He didn't know Paul. He didn't live next door to him, and he wasn't Paul's father. He was a perfect stranger--a perfect person to talk to if she could find the opportunity. She sometimes imagined her life as a movie or a story of some sort. In this episode she'd reveal the depths of her soul to her driving instructor and he'd reciprocate with an even more surprising revelation about himself: illegal alien; political asylum; new identity in the witness protection program; a single father with a crippled daughter. They'd get close, become friends, help each other out, live happily ever after in continual, ever more profound bon amie.

The movie ends with a dinner, clinking glasses of wine; the husband is functional and appreciative of all life has to offer; the crippled daughter is learning to walk on her own. Jacob, the star, at Claire's side passes rolls to everyone by joyfully, mischievously, tossing one to each person at the table. Everybody laughs.

Just as they drove past Belle Creek Park, as Claire wound up her reverie, a squirrel ran into the road in front of the car. Claire screamed, heard, then felt, the blump blump under the car, then she screeched to a stop. Jeronimo made her pull over to the side of the road. They both got out of the car. A pulpy, bubbling red line extended about ten feet behind the right rear wheel, where it seems the squirrel had lodged at exactly the moment Claire hit the break.

"Wow," said Jeronimo. "Creamed." He saw Claire was shaken. "It's okay," he said. "Common. It happens all the time."

He made a motion that meant "let's go," got back in the car on the passenger's side, and made her drive back to E-Z School. She braved the ride back, but by the time she'd parked her face was smeared with tears. She stepped out of the car quickly. As she walked away, Jeronimo called out after her, and she turned to look at him through her blur of tears. He was almost laughing. "It really is okay." She turned toward home, and did not turn around again when she heard him yell, "You did not break any laws."

Every once in a while Claire tuned in to hear her husband's voice on the radio, but she couldn't stand it for too long. She didn't care for the constant repetition of the songs, and the wacko factor got her down. Today, in Paul's absence, they played one of a series of his old tapes.

"This is Bonny Boy, Wacko Paul Bonny comin' at you with the hits, all the hits, all the time on WFIV FM Detroit with ten more than the top forty--that's fifty for all you people in remedial math. That's right forty plus ten equals fifty! The top fifty songs from no one else but me straight to only, and especially, you. And you. Okay, and you too. Uh-yeah, you too. OKAY! Let's get started!"

Paul's job didn't require him to have a personality, it required him to be a personality. Paul was a fine actor, so acting wacky was no problem, but Claire blamed his moods on the backlash from having to be wacky all day long, every day: all wacky, all the time.

She listened to the tape and attempted to discern small oddities that may have predicted his crashes, but his performances were solid. She had to mine her memory for clues of strange or quirky behavior. The first couple of times, he had developed strange relationships to odd items, toilet paper the most notable in Claire's memory. He tore through plastic wrappings in the supermarket to test the softness of the paper, and even if satisfied enough to buy it, he began to talk about his experiences with it, and how those experiences might be improved with certain types of moisturizers, or cleansers. He would take his own roll of toilet paper with them if they were invited out, and make Claire carry it in her purse.

He had once become obsessed with time. They'd been invited to a party of one of his colleagues and were told the party would start around eight o'clock. Paul ranted and raved to get to the party at exactly eight. Once outside the house, seeing no other cars, he realized that exactly eight o'clock was far too early again. He'd driven around the block ten or twelve times, slowly, suddenly patient as a fly strip, before they parked and finally went in, the third guests to arrive, at eight-twenty.

Of course everyone had quirks, and these quirks of Paul's would have been more charming than anything else for Claire, except she recalled that the quirks rose to a fervent pitch just prior to his moods, and then, when the mood passed, the quirks all but vanished.

Before the last episode they had gone to another party. The hostess told them they could put their coats in the bedroom. The bed was piled high with coats lying every which way on top of each other. Claire threw her coat on the bed and turned to see Paul standing at the opened closet door.

"What are you doing?" she asked him.

"Trying to find a hanger."

"It's their closet, Paul. You shouldn't be opening other people's closet doors."

"My coat," he said. He held it on one crooked finger. Claire gestured to the bed covered in coats.

"I'm not putting my coat there." He chose a hanger, moved aside some of the clothes, and hung up his coat.

"Nobody here is dirty, Paul."

"Still," he said. "It's not our bed." He sniffed the air, scrunched up his nose, and pushed the clothes in the closet further away on each side of his coat, so that it hung solitary in the middle before he closed the closet door and joined the party.

Paul's boss, Dean, showed up on their doorstep on the second week of Paul's latest episode. Claire had heard Paul's colleagues describing Dean, but she'd never met him herself. He was a jackass, they said, and he had a jackass laugh. Haw-haw-haw. Seriously.

Claire opened the door to a man with a goatee that accentuated, rather than hid, his weak chin. He stood on the porch with his finger on the bell. He wore a Movado watch that was too big for him, and he kept shaking his fist in the air to reposition the watch into place on his wrist. Claire spoke to him through the screen in the door.

"Paul home?" She recognized his voice. She had spoken to him twice. Paul had told her Dean worked nine to five, and on the fourth morning of this latest mood, she'd called at nine-fifteen to explain the situation. "He just can't shake this flu. I'm sure he'll be better after the weekend." She spoke to him the second time the following Monday to say it might be a few more days.

Now she said, "Dean?" He smiled and nodded. "He's in bed," she said. "He can't get up."

"It's Claire, right?" It was odd for such a resonant voice to come out of a mouth that small, pinched in the middle with little slits of lips on either side. It was a choirboy mouth that, if opened fully, would be taller than it was wide.

"Yes," she said. "I'm Claire."

"His fans miss him, Claire."

She hadn't invited him in. She'd heard stories at parties with his co-workers about Paul's boss pulling tricks like this, visiting people at their homes when they called in sick, but she'd dismissed it as an oddity too odd to be real.

Dean raised his fist between himself and Claire, and shook the watch into place. "I just thought I'd check up on him. See if there's anything I can do. To get him back up on the pony." He pulled the reins on an imaginary pony, did a little canter, then stopped. "Maybe have a chat."

Claire held the screen door open, and let the stranger in.

Dean stepped into the living room, looked at each object the way a thief would, trying to figure out what to take and what to leave. Then he looked at Claire.

"I think it's just the flu," Claire said. "Or something."

"Claire," he said. "This is the middle of the second week, Claire." His voice boomed as if he were speaking in an auditorium with no microphone. He was dressed in an undistinguished collection of business clothes: plain brown suit coat over darker brown pants. His shoes looked as if they'd been chosen for no other reason than the speed with which they could be bought and the store exited. His posture was stick-straight, the creases in his clothes severe and unrelenting.

"Well, Claire. I'll tell you something." He paused. "But first, how you doin'? Y'okay?" He placed his hand on her arm just above her elbow as if they were old friends.

"We're in the middle of lunch here," she gestured toward the kitchen using the hand of the arm Dean had touched, effectively removing his hold on it.

"That's okay, Claire." He shook his watch, then thrust both hands into both pants pockets. He lifted himself off his heels, then set himself back down. He kept eye contact with Claire the entire time. She suspected he'd graduated in the top twenty of his Dale Carnegie course.

"Would you like something?" she said. "To eat, I mean?"

"Sure!" he said. "That'd be grand, Claire."

"All I have are sandwiches."

"That's just fine. A sandwich'd really hit the spot, matter of fact."

She gave him the choice between peanut butter and jelly, or cheese.

"Cheese, please. Just a little mayo, Claire, if you will. And some lettuce, if you have any."

She made the sandwich and poured some milk, then shooed the two older boys off to play in the backyard. She pulled Chad in his high chair over to the corner to let him play with the mess of carrots and applesauce on his tray so she could clean the table. "Let me just clean up a little, then we can talk, okay?" She motioned to Dean to sit at the table.

"Sure, Claire. Sure. Sure."

As she busied herself with the crumbs, plates, and glasses, Dean dug into his sandwich. This man, so meticulous in his carriage and gait, so peculiarly rigid and fastidious even when he stood still, was now bent over the table. Both elbows propped the sandwich less than an inch above his plate. He bent his head down repeatedly to bite the sandwich, almost like a dog at his dish. He ate loudly, chewed with his mouth open. Every once in a while he'd raise his head to the level of his glass, and with a gulp or two wash down the chewed remains of the sandwich. Claire tried not to stare at first, but in the end she couldn't help herself. The man was clearly so deeply entrenched in the world of eating his sandwich that he didn't notice Claire staring. She stood immobile in the middle of the kitchen with a wet rag full of crumbs in a hand poised carefully over her other palm.

When he finished, he straightened suddenly, wiped his mouth with the napkin, and checked his shirt and tie to make sure he hadn't stained them. His expression was that of a man waking from a deep dream. He blinked, looked around, and saw Claire.

"Fine, Claire. That was a fine sandwich." Claire flinched only slightly. He looked as if he were blushing for a moment, then grew pale again when he remembered why he'd come. He cleared his throat. "About Paul, Claire."

She sat down. "I think he'll be better soon."

Dean did not respond except to fold his napkin back into a square and smooth it with his hands onto the table.

"Is there a problem at work? I mean, is he in danger of losing his job because of this?"

"Well, certainly, Claire, we've been a little strapped since Paul's been away. We're relatively new, radio station-wise, and very small, only two years on air. Luckily we have a backlog of routines Paul recorded so the listeners don't notice. Yet. We can probably find someone to cover his shifts, if we have to. And he has insurance, but he has to see a doctor. You've taken him to a doctor?"

"No." Until she said this, it hadn't occurred to her that she'd overlooked something. Paul didn't trust doctors after his mother's experience with them. "Chicken bone, my ass," he'd once said.

"No," she repeated to Dean. Then she added, "It's just the flu. This time it hit pretty bad, but he'll be up and around in no time."

"Have you thought about...." She could tell he paused more for effect than to search for what he'd say next. "Well, I hate to say it. But.... AIDS, or something?"

"Have I thought about it?"

"AIDS. Or something. You know? I mean, how many times can you get the flu in a year?" His hands were crossed and folded in front of him on the table top as if he were at prayer.

"I don't think so," she said.

"How many times can a man get the flu in a year?" he repeated. He leaned in toward his clasped hands as if he were about to whisper, but spoke in his normal booming tone. "This is the third time in four months, Claire."

"Paul doesn't have AIDS. I assure you. It's not 1990."

"I hear people still get it, though. Has he been tested?"

"Maybe it's just a little exhaustion."

"It's just... well... he is... he's so.... creative." He let the word hang for a moment. "And... sensitive, isn't he."

Claire stared at Dean.

"It's just a thought," he said. He straightened.

They sat in awkward silence, which Claire refused to break.

"Listen, Claire. Could I talk to him?"

"That's not a good idea." She stood, collected his plate, and swept with her hand around where the plate sat, even though there were no crumbs anywhere. "If he's able, later, I'll have him call you," she paused to add extra emphasis to his name. "Dean."

She walked into the foyer and stood with her hand on the knob of the front door, so there'd be no question about where she expected Dean to go.

When Claire opened the bedroom door she found Paul filing the calloused skin of his feet with a pumice stone. He had made the bed and lay on top of the purple bedspread. He said he'd heard them talking and not to worry. "I'm really sorry for all this, Claire. I'll call Dean when I'm through here." The filings of dead skin fell in a white powder all around him. When he finally got up to call Dean, the purple bedspread showed the silhouette of his trunk, pelvis, and the tops of his legs outlined in a chalky dust.

That night, Paul ate half a sandwich and half an apple pie from McDonald's that Robert refused to eat.

The next morning at four-thirty Claire was up and working at the computer as usual when she heard Paul get up. He ate a bowl of Cheerios, took a shower, and cut his hair down to the nub except for a little tuft in front. After the unwashed tangle of bedhead hair perched atop the mute staring creature of the previous week, Claire couldn't help but be more relieved than alarmed. His hair and body were clean, his eyes looked at Claire when he spoke. He spoke!

"I feel better," he told her. He kissed her on the top of her head, and went to work.

Claire listened to his show to see if she could perceive any sudden, if subtle, differences. If Paul had lost his verve, his radio personality didn't show it. If anything, he was louder, more ebullient and obnoxious than ever.

"Howdy Do Detroit! It's Bonny Boy Wacko Paul Bonny, coming back at you full throttle with the hits!"

His voice was again deep and resonant with wacko. She turned the radio off and got the boys up at around ten o'clock. At noon, the phone rang.

"Mrs. Bonny?"

It was Paul's boss, Dean.

"Claire? You need to come get Paul. There's something wrong. He's crying and he won't stop."

"I don't have a car."

"Look," Dean said. His tone had changed. He was no longer lubricious and smarmy. He scolded her like a child. "I have to handle the situation here." He emphasized the "I" to prove himself a beleaguered soul, the one always stuck with other people's shit and damn well sick of it. "Otherwise I could come to get you, but that's not possible. You need to find a ride. If you can't find anyone, I may be able to get someone to fetch you, but it is not likely. Call me back in ten minutes to let me know what you're going to do."

She didn't know what to do. She called her father-in-law, determined to tell him everything that had been happening. But when he answered the phone she could only say his name. "Jonathan?"

His voice, hollow and old, caught on the one syllable of her name, then quieted. She knew she'd never spill the whole story over the phone, and decided to simply go and get Paul, and let Jonathan see for himself. Then they could all deal with it together.

"Jonathan, Paul's sick and I have to go pick him up at work."

"Oh," he said.

"I'm going to have a friend drive me, can you watch the kids?"

"I can drive you," he said. He sounded, as usual, beaten, uncertain.

"I've already called my friend."

"Okay."

"Be here in a few minutes?"

"Sure. Ten minutes."

She hung up and called Jeronimo. Jeronimo picked up in the middle of the first ring. She asked for an "emergency lesson," and asked that he pick her up.

It was twelve-fifteen when Jeronimo screeched to a stop in front of her house. The sun was small, white, high in the sky, and scorching. Jeronimo stepped out of the car to get into the passenger's seat, as usual. Claire, only half out the front door called out, "No. You drive." When she got in the car she told him, "I'm sorry. I lied, but I didn't know what else to do. I don't need a lesson, I need a ride to my husband's work. Here." She gave him directions, handed him forty dollars. "But the emergency part is true."

"You don't have to pay me," he said, but stuffed the bills into his jeans pocket anyway.

The car didn't start or stop without a jerk and a screech. He chose the busiest lanes, rode the tail of every car in front of him, and cursed unspellable curses.

"We don't have to speed," she said. "There's no need to rush too much. We can just drive normally."

"I am driving normally," he told her. His face was relaxed and pleasant except when he swore. He turned up the radio and sang. Feel the beat of the rhythm of the night.... His voice may have been a song when he spoke, but when he sang, it was a torture chamber of half-whispered screeches and howls. He paid no heed to the white lines that marked the lanes, drifted to and fro, hither and yon without care. He squeezed between cars in other lanes when there was barely room to sneeze between the bumpers. He looked happy. Even when he suddenly cut off a huge semi truck and brought the driver's wrath, in the form of the fierce bellow of the foghorn sounding blast, down upon them, Jeronimo only sang louder. The beat. The beat.

Jeronimo pulled into the radio station's lot and told Claire he'd find a place to park and wait for her. Claire told him no. "My husband has his car here," she said. Wobbly in the knees and queasy, she took the elevator up to the station on the sixth floor.

Paul sat in a room silently crying. She'd expected sobs and noise, so she was relieved.

"I think you should take him to the emergency room," Dean told her.

Dean's back was to Paul. Paul looked up at Claire and shook his head no.

"We'll see," she said. Paul grabbed her arm and walked her out into the hall. He refused to ride the elevator, so they walked down the six flights of stairs.

Once outside in the lot Paul offered to drive, but Claire forced him to give her the keys. He was still crying. "If we're stopped I can show them my permit," she told him.

"No hospital," he said when they got into the car. "Just go home. Please. One more day. All I need is one more day." He breathed heavily to try to subdue his crying. A snot bubble grew, then exploded under his nose. He wiped it away with his long fingers, then onto his jeans. "I went back too soon, is all. Tomorrow I'll be fine, I swear." He said all this quietly, then, loudly, forcefully, almost frantically, he said, "I swear, Claire. I swear it! I'll be fine tomorrow."

"Paul," she said. "I think maybe we should. We're closer to the hospital than we are to the house anyway."

"I knew it. You hate me," he said quietly. He clenched his fists and rested them on his knees. "I don't blame you, I don't blame you at all. You should hate me. But." He had to collect the energy and the breath to finish his thought. "Don't put me away." His mouth stretched obscenely, involuntarily prolonging the word "away" in his unsuccessful attempt to keep from sobbing. In his wide open mouth, in the middle of "away," a white line of spit connected the top teeth with the bottom.

She leaned over him, leaned her arm on his thigh, and realized how boney he was. He must have lost at least ten pounds in the past two weeks. She found a package of tissues in the glove compartment and handed it to him. "You're being ridiculous."

"This proves it, Claire. Why won't you believe me? I said I'd be better by tomorrow." Claire sat back, watched Paul cry, and tried to figure out what to do, where to go. His whole body trembled. After a few moments, he shifted slowly out of his own private world of misery, and seemed to be aware of Claire watching him. He pulled his hands up to his face, and Claire thought this might be the dam breaking, her way out to take him to the hospital without blaming herself for unusual cruelty. But he simply wiped the tears from his eyes and rubbed his face as if he were washing it with a washcloth. He wiped his hands on his jeans and, although he sat perfectly still, Claire saw the extreme effort with which he attempted to pull himself together. Every muscle in his face and neck slowly hardened into a pose he seemed to have memorized, and with which he knew the world and Claire might be familiar.

Suddenly he sat up straight. He was quiet while Claire started the car. When she put it into gear, he wiped the last tears from his eyes, blew his nose, and sighed a sigh as if he'd run a marathon.

"Actually," he said. "I'm feeling much better already." He rolled down the window and let the summer air refresh him. "Much better." He laughed. "Whew." He leaned his head back against the headrest and turned to look at Claire.

"Seriously, Claire. Let's just go home, I'll take a nap, we'll have dinner and talk about it, okay? I know I've put you through a lot. Maybe I do need some help. But we should talk about it first, don't you think?" He sounded like himself again, but Claire was afraid to take her eyes off the road to look at him.

"Okay," she said. "Okay okay okay. For now. But obviously something big is wrong. Right?"

Paul was silent.

"Right?"

"I guess," he said.

Claire felt she'd won something, but it was a cheap victory over a helpless man. She capitulated a little.

"Maybe talking to someone will help. If you're not better tomorrow, we'll call for an appointment, okay?"

Paul remained silent.

"Paul. Say okay or I'm driving to the emergency room right now."

"Okay!" he said.

"Okay."

By the time they reached the house, Paul looked a bit weary, but was completely composed.

"You look like you could use some rest," Jonathan said.

"Yeah," said Paul. "I'm a little worn out, is all." Paul's clothes hung off him like rags on a tree.

"Get your hair cut?" Jonathan said.

"Yeah."

"Kinda short."

"I s'pose. It's just hair. It'll grow back."

"Looks okay," Jonathan conceded. He patted Paul on the shoulder. "You go take a nap. I'll see you all later."

"Thanks Dad," Paul said.

For the rest of the evening he was better. He ate supper. Afterwards, he played the guitar for the boys, and sang. The boys sat rapt, dutifully in a row on the floor in front of Paul. Robert watched Paul's hands to see how he plucked the strings. Joseph studied Paul's face and tried to relax into the reemergence of his father back into their lives.

Claire watched Paul too. She watched his long fingers conjure beauty from the guitar. His adam's apple, normally prominent in his long neck, was even more pronounced. She often kissed him there when they made love. Now it bobbed up and down like a knot in a rope on a pulley. This man had given her more joy than she'd ever expected or hoped for, and she could not return the favor to him. She saw that here, surrounded by his family, he was utterly alone. There was no way to touch him, and nothing she could do to help him.

The more he sang, the closer he seemed to get to tears again. She stood up to stop him from going too far in front of the boys. She wrapped her arms around him from behind and put her hands on the guitar. To her surprise, he set the guitar down quickly and swung around to her. He was still sitting, she standing, and he hugged her waist hard. He clung to her like a child and wouldn't let go. Claire was trapped, her husband's arms clamped around her waist, her hands on his head and shoulder, the boys still sitting in their row, watching as if it were part of the show.

"Bedtime," Claire said. The boys got up and began to get themselves ready. Paul didn't move, but he didn't cry again. He squeezed her hard, and trembled.

Later, Paul even made an attempt at sex, but the effort dissolved after the first few moments into a snuggle, which was still closer than they'd been in over a month. There'd been sexual ebbs in the past too. She sensed it coming on days when he'd make halfhearted efforts to play with the kids after work, but then hole himself up alone in the bedroom listening to the violin sonatas of Sarasate over and over again. His particular favorite was a malagueña, and Claire now regretted the times she purposely slammed closed doors and drawers whenever she heard the first whining strings of it. During these spells the sex dropped off completely. At tip-top, Paul was playful, growling, aggressive and funny during sex, which still occurred occasionally. Claire had attributed the waning frequency to everything she'd heard about marriage after children, even though she'd been lucky: her pregnancies had only softened her skinny edges instead of deforming her into the bloated mess other women complained about having become.

The next morning, he got up early again. Claire asked him if he was sure he wouldn't see a doctor.

"I'm fine," he told her. "Really." He kissed her, told her he loved her, and left again for work.

Paul had brought his laptop to work with a playlist of ten hours of his own selection of no-format, off-the-beaten-track favorites that ranged from old jazz to punk to bubble gum rock to spirituals to show tunes to Motown.

He queued up the music himself, waved to his tech, stepped out of his sound booth, locked it, trotted down the six flights of stairs, left the building, ran across the almost vacant parking lot, across the two lanes of Schoolcraft road, climbed over the short fence there and continued down the parched slope of the grassy embankment to the highway and out onto the six lanes of westbound I-96 morning traffic. In the second of the six lanes, his body met the body of a red pickup truck driven by a nineteen-year-old boy on his way to the second day at his new job as a motel desk clerk. There was some swerving and screeching of tires, but the traffic at that time of the morning was relatively light. The drivers of the few other cars on the road remained spectators and witnesses rather than participants in this event. The driver of the red pickup truck was shaken, but unharmed in body.

Nobody was hurt except Paul, who, at the hospital thirty minutes later, was pronounced dead on arrival.

Except for the whirr of the sprinklers here and there, the slight scratching of squirrels' nails against the bark of trees, the low electric buzz of fans and air conditioners, the neighborhood was quiet. The three days of furious activity that follows a sudden death were almost at an end. The black suits and dresses of mourners, soggy from summer sweat and disconsolate tears, had been hung in closets, or draped over chairs, or heaped in a pile to wait for the owners, or the owners' mother, to fold or hang in anticipation of the next occasion, or only to get them out of sight.

Claire slept.

The boys were with Jonathan and Paul's sister, Denise, at Jonathan's house. The neighbors had brought over more food than three families could eat in a month. Claire had had Dean announce that after the burial, after people had a chance to rest and change into everyday comfortable clothes, that everyone was welcome to come back to Claire's house at 4 PM, ("no sooner than 4 PM, please") to help eat the food. Claire had asked Denise to take the kids so she could be alone for a little bit to straighten up the house.

Instead, she turned off the phone, and slept.

Claire had fallen asleep pondering the word "suicide," the way it sounded so abstract, the way it fooled her. In her own private vocabulary, the word was always accompanied by the modifier "attempted," which suggested failure, and implied hope.

In sleep, her mind bounced back and forth and up and down among ambiguities. When she woke, she was aware mostly of the effect of gravity pulling her body down into the cushions and springs of the living room couch. She felt rested but a little sea sick, as if she'd slept on the bottom of a boat with a hundred heavy tarpaulins over her.

She peeled her body upright into a sitting position on the couch, placed her bare feet on the carpet to get her land legs. Within a few moments she managed to stand, to walk, to turn the fans in both bedroom windows at the back of the house on high, and to take a shower to rinse away the sweat and tears and sleep. The breeze that swirled through the house dried her; she took her time walking naked through the house, pulled on one of Paul's t-shirts, and her cutoff shorts. She had about fifteen minutes before people would arrive. Her wet hair cooled her back as the water soaked through the shirt.

A light sound of metal clattering against metal moved through the house, coming in over the blades of the fans in the back windows with the rhythms of a machine.

One more minute, Claire prayed to herself. One more minute alone.

She sat at the head of the kitchen table facing the windows. The drawn shades lifted and fell with the incoming breeze, and she saw bits of the afternoon: a patch of lawn, a glint of sun off an edge of metal somewhere, on something.

The clatter behind the house stopped. From the front porch a different noise sounded: the scratch of metal on cement, the squeak of someone sitting in the lawn chair. Claire surrendered.

She opened the living room drapes to see who was on the porch, and what was left of the afternoon. Jacob sat in the lawn chair.

"Hi," he said to her when she came out to sit in the chair next to his.

"Hi," she said. The porch's cement was warm on her bare feet.

"Grandma's getting ready for the party at your house."

Claire tousled his hair. Jacob reached up and fixed his hair back the way it was. The sun had sifted down to rest over the tops of the tall trees planted in the suburban blocks that stretched to the west in front of them to Merriman Road.

"Grandma says I can't play in the pool because it's a sad party."

"It's a going away party," Claire told him. "My husband went away."

Jacob picked his nose and put the booger on the bottom of his sandal. "That's why we can't play in the pool?"

"We'll see," Claire said. She looked at Jacob. "Will you sit here, on my lap?"

He slid down off his chair and into Claire's lap so that they both faced the trees with the sun hovering over their branches. His skin was so smooth!

"I don't see why we can't get the pool out," she said. "It's my house. We can do whatever we want."

Beauty opened her screen door a crack and leaned her head out. "Jacob!" she said. "I told you not to go over there yet."

"He's keeping me company," Claire said. "This boy is like magic on me."

"Oh," said Beauty. She stepped fully onto the porch. "We've got some stuff to bring over. You just tell us when you're ready."

Claire hugged Jacob closer and smelled his hair. If I could sit like this all night, I'd be happy, is what she wanted to say.

"I'm ready," she said.

Beauty disappeared for a moment into the house, then returned followed by Estelle. Estelle carried a case of red wine, Beauty carried a case of white. They all walked around to the backyard together, where row upon row of lawn chairs stood folded against the fence.

Beauty unpacked the bottles of white wine into a metal tub that she had also hoisted over the fence while Claire was sleeping. "I didn't know how many people would be here," she said. She bit off the corner of plastic on a bag of ice that she'd also set in the yard, then ripped it open spilling it into the metal tub filled with white wine bottles, then into a second tub filled with beer. "Judging from the crowd today, it'll be a lot." She jerked her head in the direction of the lawn furniture. "I brought extra chairs."

Everyone arrived all at once, at fifteen minutes after four. At least a hundred people, all carrying more food. Claire filled the pool and let the kids play until the food had

been spread out onto the picnic table and card tables
Beauty had also foreseen to acquire. It was a lovely afternoon: clear and dry, warm, but cooling. Claire's children
flocked around Jonathan. They came to Denise when
they wanted a hamburger. Chad clung to his grandfather
like a leech. People kept arriving in droves: friends and
neighbors and relatives Claire had heard of, but never
met, or met once, along with many other familiar faces
she had difficulty assigning names to.

It was hard to keep of track of anything. After making
sure everyone had something to eat and utensils and
napkins and a beverage, Estelle and Beauty sat down
to eat. Jacob immediately ran over to Estelle clutching
the bottom of his pants.

"Is he okay?" Claire asked.

"Potty time," smirked Estelle. She looked for a place
to set her potato salad. Claire offered to take Jacob to
the bathroom for her.

"No, don't be silly," Estelle said.

"You don't be silly," said Claire. "Look at everything
you've done. Eat. It'll give me a chance to use the new
potty we got for Joseph. He doesn't use it as much as
he should."

Jacob shivered in the cool late afternoon breeze, so
Claire found his t-shirt and brought it in with them. On
the potty, he amazed her again. Without embarrassment
he pooped, plop, plop, and let her wipe him without any
fuss. He asked Claire for a boost to the sink so he could
wash his hands by himself.

Instead of going out the back door into the crowd,
Claire walked out onto her front porch to get a breath of

air. She hadn't expected him to, but when Jacob followed her out onto the porch, she was happy. She took a deep breath, and sighed. Jacob imitated her. Paul's car sat in front of the house in the same place Jonathan had left it after bringing it home after "the accident," as Denise and Jonathan called it.

Claire looked at Jacob. "Want to go for a ride?" she asked.

Jacob nodded.

Driving on the expressway was easier than driving on the city streets, so as soon as she could, Claire got onto westbound I-96. She drove the route she had sometimes driven with Jeronimo. The turn onto I-275 where she usually merged to the right and headed back north came up with comforting familiarity, but Claire decided to keep going straight instead. She had no idea where she was going or when she would stop.

Soon the city fell behind them. Open fields and rows of plowed land didn't seem possible so close to Detroit, but then so much that once seemed impossible turned out closer than Claire would ever have guessed.

The afternoon sun had lost its edge, but Claire still had to keep the visor down and squint as she pointed out horses and cows to Jacob. Mostly they rolled along next to long stretches of empty fields, but when she saw that occasionally the highway split off in three separate directions Claire made small choices, opting most often for straight ahead. This is what it was like to ride off into the sunset. Claire laughed for the first time in days, and it felt good.

She saw a sign for Ann Arbor, which she'd visited only once with Paul right before Robert was born. She thought she remembered she liked it.

The signs led her right into the heart of the downtown.

"Are you hungry again?" she asked Jacob.

"I am hUUUUngry!" he said.

"Me too."

This child frightened her. He had no cares or worries in the world. She knew his affection for her was not specific; he had the charisma of playboys and dictators--he couldn't help it. She feared his charisma would become an affliction for him, as her general state of resilient happiness had for her.

There were no places to park on the street. The parking garage loomed, complicated and forbidding on her left. She slowed the car and pulled over, idling with her emergency lights blinking to see how other drivers did it. She watched three cars. When no other cars were on the street, she went for it, pressed on the gas to propel herself up the ramp enough to get to the gate without ramming into it. She had misjudged the distance from the booth, and had to park, and step out to get the ticket from the automated dispenser. She slowly pulled in and readjusted her eyes from the bright outdoor light to the dank darkness of the garage, and in the meantime another car pulled in behind her.

The guy behind her was in a rush and kept honking his horn, but she couldn't go any faster over the bumpy ramps. Finally she found an area on the fourth level with no cars where she parked without much trouble, only having to back in and out of the spot twice to get the car straight. She memorized her spot and took Jacob's hand to walk down the stairs and back out into the light.

Jacob held Claire's hand the whole time. They strolled through the faux-bohemian enclave of the university town in the calm of the coming evening as if there were no place else to be or to go, as if nothing very upsetting were happening anywhere in the world.

Jacob looked everywhere at once, equally enthralled by the street musicians, the mangoes in a fruit stand, the parking meters that cast shadows on the ground that looked like the silhouette of a Mickey Mouse head. The town was more sparse than during the normal academic year, but the streets were still lively. Flowing-skirted girls flirted with army booted, mohawk-haired boys who seemed oblivious that their look inspired a faint nostalgia in someone Claire's age rather than the shock effect Claire supposed they were going for.

Claire and Jacob strolled and watched people. There were worried looking nerds, clean-smelling young men, some older, rumpled, vaguely professorial types. At a Middle Eastern café Claire indulged her craving for hummus, tabouli, and babaganoush. Unlike any of her children, who cried if an unfamiliar dish was even set in front of them, Jacob tried all three. He liked the hummus and the tabouli, but not the babaganoush.

A block or so down, across from a Rastafarian selling incense, they stopped for ice cream. Jacob asked for "white," but when he saw the green of Claire's pistachio ice cream, he wanted that too, and they took turns licking each other's cones. The girl who served them the ice cream saw Claire trying to wipe off the stickiness from her fingers and Jacob's face, and pointed to a spray bottle filled with water next to a roll of paper towels standing on end next to it. "Our hand washing station," the girl said. Claire squirted down herself and Jacob, cleaned up, and continued their tour.

For half an hour or so, Claire and Jacob sat on a sloped sprawling lawn in front of a huge stone building to watch a hackysack game among shirtless men not yet twenty years old. The athletic arcs of their bodies were a pure kind of beauty. The muscles in the boys' shoulders, backs, and legs flexed and twitched as the hackysack ball, continually kicked and perpetually spinning, bobbed between the feet and bodies of the boys.

Finally, Claire stood up and held out her hand. Jacob had been transfixed by the game, and wanted to stay.

"Time to go," she said. He stood, and held her hand as they walked away, but he looked back for the length of the whole block. One of the boys waved to him. Claire and Jacob both waved back, then turned the corner to find the car.

It was enough. These five senses and her interactions with certain other people were enough to keep her happy. Why hadn't it been enough for Paul? It was all enough: the spring night breezing in through the opened car windows ruffling Jacob's hair, the pretentious buffoon on the classical music station opining in some elitist jargon that Claire found hilarious. Even the feel of the steering wheel under her hands was beautiful, as was the feeling in her throat and on her tongue when she spoke to Jacob once the car got rolling again and up to speed with the rest of the cars on the expressway.

"People might blame me," she said, "for what happened to Paul."

Both windows were rolled down, so she had to yell to hear herself. The wind coming in through the windows whipped her hair around her face and neck. Sometimes she had to reach up to remove a strand or two that had caught in her mouth while she spoke.

"Everybody gets sad, don't they? You get sad sometimes too," she shouted. "Don't you?"

She didn't feel confident enough yet to take her eyes off the road to look at him, but she shifted her eyes quickly to the side to see if she could catch a movement like a nod in her peripheral vision. As far as she could tell, Jacob was looking for more cows.

"Of course you do," she said. She had passed the few other cars that were on the road, and now had no gauge by which she could pace herself. She refused to look at the speedometer. She pressed harder on the gas pedal, just see how it felt.

It felt good.

"I never thought...." It was seven-thirty; they still had at least an hour more of sun. The shadows of the large trees that fringed the fields lengthened to cover large stretches of orange and yellow sun-dappled prairie grass in swatches of blue and green shade.

"What do you think of all this, Jacob?"

Jacob yelled over the sound of the wind rushing through the car, "I liked that man with the dog who played the music with his mouth."

"Harmonica," she yelled back. "That's called a harmonica."

"Yeah," he said.

She stole a quick look at him. The wind blew his hair straight back. He leaned his head back against the seat as if he were going to sleep soon.

With the wind blowing on her face and the events of the past few days having pulled so many tears from her, she couldn't cry anymore if she'd wanted to. She said to the wind, "It's not a crime to be happy." She beat her fist on the steering wheel and the horn sounded.

Jacob said, "WOOO!"

Claire said, "That's right, WOOOOO!" She honked the horn again. And again. And again.

Until Jacob knelt on the seat, she hadn't realized she'd forgotten about the car seat, or to buckle him in with the regular seat belt. He leaned both hands on the window with his face pressed against the incoming wind. "WOOOOO!"

Claire, also seatbeltless, echoed him. "WOOOOO!"

The senseless, satisfying howl swept them through the evening, and the small decisions Claire made while driving led them, in their small, unbuckled freedom, home. With the windows down, the engine hummed and the friction of the tires spun off the roar of the world, replaced it with the pleasingly high howl of hay and manure scented wind crashing through the opened windows.

She talked to Jacob the way she'd never been able to talk to Jeronimo, certainly never to Jonathan or Denise, the way she'd wanted to talk to Estelle. She kept talking as they rolled toward home away from the sun, past the farms and fields into the long stretches of concrete nothingness that marked these suburbs. The closer she got to home, the heavier the traffic grew. When the rural faded into the suburban, the highway dipped into the ground, where it was shouldered by smaller service drives which gave off onto larger main streets, each with three lanes of traffic going each way. The traffic slowed.

"Paul once asked me, 'Is that all life is? Keeping busy?'"

The noise of the traffic and the wind still purred through the car. Jacob slept.

"No," Claire continued. She quieted for a moment. "He didn't love me enough. Or he didn't believe me when I told him how much I loved him. Or, maybe, he didn't care. Enough, anyway." The wind and the traffic died down, and Claire clearly heard her own voice again saying, "I don't know I don't know I don't know," until the words blurred and lost both sense and meaning, and then she stopped talking.

Her hair settled from the frenzied whipping to a mild riffling across her face and over her neck as she pulled off the expressway at her exit. Her face was hot from where the wind had whirled over it. Her ears rang. She was almost home. She stopped at a traffic light. The sudden quiet woke Jacob.

Something was happening on the road: an unusual kind of activity in the traffic near Seven Mile Road and Merriman. Although there wasn't much traffic, the cars on the road crowded Claire's, and crowded her even more when she turned onto her street.

Jacob sat up in his seat. He pointed at the police cars that lined their street. When the unmarked car behind her turned on the flashing lights, Jacob pointed with his finger, "Look."

"I know," Claire told him. She knew there was more love in the world for Jacob and for her and for her children than any of them could ever support or stand or return. It was as fierce and real as gravity, and had pulled all of these people here swirling around her tonight. She did what she never thought she'd be able to do while driving: she turned her head, taking her eyes off the road just for a few seconds to smile at Jacob. "Everything is okay, Jacob," she said, and despite what she knew of the world she believed that what she'd said was true, for the moment. She returned her eyes to the road, but reached over with her right hand to stroke his hair.

"It's okay," she repeated. "They're looking for us, and we're here."

The unmarked car edged up closer behind her. Over the loudspeaker, a voice told her to pull over, but she still had another block to go. As they escorted her home she saw, from a block away, Jonathan and Denise, Estelle and Beauty watch the approaching convoy with her in the lead.

The loudspeaker voice told her, "Pull over. Now," in a tone that did not sound very friendly. Claire slowed a little, but kept going.

It was a beautiful evening. The light fell on the street the same way it had on the night she first met Paul when they'd left the party together to get beer.

That night! It was a typical summer dusk in midtown Manhattan. They'd stepped out onto Fifty-second Street. On their left, their shadows lay down like cats stretching almost to Eighth Avenue. Their shadows went one way and the sun went the other. To their right, the sun worked its way down the sky over the Hudson into New Jersey and beyond. She could see it now, here: Livonia, that's where the sun went. It was the same sun, she could almost feel it was the same night, except that now so much was new, so much old, so much gone. But she'd been happy. That night, on the way to the liquor store, Paul and Claire walked with their backs to the sun, their long shadows shimmering before them. They bought two bottles of red wine, and no beer. By the time they walked back west, intending to return to the party, she saw the sun, the day slithering away across the river to who knew where. They didn't know yet that they'd bypass the party, go back to Claire's apartment three blocks away with the intention of bringing real wine glasses back to the party to avoid drinking wine out of cheap plastic cups. They didn't know they wouldn't get back to the party at all that night, that they'd drink the wine themselves, stay up talking all night on the futon in Claire's studio apartment, fall asleep in each others' arms, then wake and make love for the first time the next morning. They didn't know or think about what came before or what might come after.

All they knew was this: sweet summer dusk on Fifty-second Street; the lazy fat cat in the second hand store on the corner drowsing in the blade of sun that fell across the window; Ninth Avenue burning in the fading sun; their joy at turning onto lovely, tree-lined Fifty-fifth Street, where the leaves shivered in their own shade in response to the breeze coming off the river; the streets almost empty because of the weekend holiday; the eerie feeling that they'd been singled out for each other; they knew the joy of being alive—here, now, with each other—and that they had the whole long night before them.

Claire parked the car in front of her house. To show her good will to Estelle, to Beauty, to Jonathan, to Denise and to all the policemen who now surrounded her car, she waved, one hand high in the air first, and then the other.

The bodies of the policemen that opened the car door for her blocked the view of her home and family, but above their heads Claire watched the light in the sky changing from dusk to night: odd blues, oranges, yellows, reds bled into each other and darkened, threatened by the white and blue and red of the flashing squad lights. She saw the tips of the pine and the maple in her own backyard rise above her house. Someone turned off the squad lights. The quarter moon in the southeast sky rested among a few bright stars. The large, gentle hand of the policeman who held her arm was warm and dry. In the oak at the end of the block the starlings, all aflutter again in the still air, clacked and chattered wild greetings through the fresh evening as it ripened to purple night, into which Claire stepped lightly.

Acknowledgments

I would like to thank the entire staff at Cornerstone Press for their help in getting these stories into shape, as well as the many editors who helped shape these stories as they first appeared in literary magazines.

For encouragement of my development as a writer, I thank Connie Brothers, Frank Conroy, Michael Cunningham, Eileen Donovan-Kranz, James Allen McPherson, Marilynne Robinson, Lad Tobin, and Jessica Treadway. I am deeply grateful to every writer at the Iowa Writers' Workshop who had the patience and good will to read and comment on some of these stories as I was cooking them up.

I'm also eternally grateful to the owners of the many cafés who allowed the weird guy in the corner to sit and stare for hours on end while he scratched intermittently in his notebook, especially Francine D'Olimpio of Francesca's in Boston, the staff at The Java House in Iowa City, and Jen Greenberg of Grounded in New York.

I owe thanks for financial support to Houghton Mifflin for a Houghton Mifflin Literary Fellowship; the J. Willard and Alice S. Marriott Foundation for the generous gift of an Alice Sheets Grant; and the Copernicus Society of America for a Michener-Copernicus Fellowship.

And, most particularly, I thank Derek Fox, for everything.

Gratefully acknowledged are the following publications in which some of these stories first appeared:

"Exiles" appeared in *Alaska Quarterly Review*
"The Collector" appeared in *Santa Monica Review*
"Great Escapes from Detroit" appeared in *Santa Monica Review*
"Too Beautiful" appeared in *The Chariton Review*
"H.O.M.E.S." appeared in *American Literary Review*
"Proof" appeared in *Carolina Quarterly*